Praise for *How to Ruin a Summer Vacation*

"…book is sure to please readers looking for a fun read that
also digs deeper into complex emotions."—*KLIATT*

"Funny, sharp dialogue keeps the teen conversations fresh
and true to life."—*SLJ* *"Remarkable Reads"*

"Simone Elkeles has a terrific voice and
a terrific heroine in Amy!"
—*Jennifer Crusie, co-author of* Don't Look Down

OTHER BOOKS BY SIMONE ELKELES

SIMONE ELKELES

How to Ruin My Teenage Life

flux™
Woodbury, Minnesota

First Edition
Seventh Printing, 2013

Book design by Steffani Sawyer
Cover design by Lisa Novak
Cover image © iStockphoto.com / Lóránd Gelner
Editing by Rhiannon Ross

Flux, an imprint of Llewellyn Publications

Library of Congress Cataloging-in-Publication Data
How to ruin my teenage life / Simone Elkeles. — 1st ed.
    p. cm.
ISBN: 978-0-7387-1019-8
 [1. Identity--Fiction. 2. Jews--United States--Fiction. 3. Israelis--United States--Fiction. 4. Interpersonal relations--Fiction. 5. Schools--Fiction. 6. Fathers and daughters--Fiction. 7. Chicago (Ill.)--Fiction.]
I. Title.

PZ7.E42578Ht 2007
 [Fic]--dc22
                                2007005535

Flux
Llewellyn Publications
A Division of Llewellyn Worldwide Ltd.
2143 Wooddale Drive
Woodbury, MN 55125-2989
www.fluxnow.com

Printed in the United States of America

Dedication

For Samantha

my daughter…
my companion…
my friend…
You'll always be a princess in my eyes

Acknowledgments

I'd like to thank Nadia Cornier, my agent who is the epitome of the term "full-service agent."

Andrew Karre has been an amazing editor whose advice I totally respect and count on—thank you for believing in my stories even when I changed the endings after you bought them. I've had a great time working with the entire Flux family (Brian Farrey, Rhiannon Ross, Amy Martin, and Lisa Novak). What an incredible team I've had behind me!

My friend Karen Harris has been there for me for years, guiding me when my own flashlight in life is dim. (And when I'm stuck in a scene I can always count on you to pull me out.) You are the definition of a forever friend.

Lisa Laing's book trailers bring my books to life on my website—thank you so much for your friendship and talent!

I wouldn't be a published author today without Romance Writers of America and especially my local chapter, Chicago-North RWA. It's true that romance writers have the biggest hearts.

Last but not least, a huge thanks to Samantha, Brett and Moshe for being supportive and understanding when I needed it most. My family is my lifeline.

1

My name is Amy Nelson-Barak. My mom is a Nelson and my dad is a Barak. And no, they were never married. Being an illegitimate kid used to freak me out, but I guess this past summer when my Israeli dad took me to his homeland I got over it.

Mom got married a few months ago to Marc *"with a c."* He's okay, I guess, if you like the über-conservative type. They moved to the 'burbs after the wedding, as if marriage somehow warrants moving to a place where you have to drive a car to get to the nearest Starbucks.

I'm living with my father in Chicago. I call him *Aba*, which means Dad in Hebrew. He owns this cool condo in a building in Chicago on the fortieth floor. He was pretty non-existent in my life up until a few months ago. To make a long story short, this past summer my dad and I got to know each other and worked out our issues. He's learning how to be a dad to a teenage girl (me) and I'm learning how to deal with an overprotective father. I've decided to live with him until I graduate high school so I don't have to change schools. The best part about his place is it's situated directly next to a coffee shop called Perk Me Up! It's like a Starbucks, only it has better coffee.

Okay, so I don't *exactly* drink coffee. I just turned seventeen in December and haven't gotten that acquired taste thing goin' on. But that's not the point. I'm a city girl. And a coffee shop steps away from your front door equals city.

I'm sitting at Perk Me Up! right now, doing algebra homework on this frosty January day. Winter break ended a week ago, but I'm still struggling to get into the swing of things at school. I could go upstairs and study in a quiet place, but since my dad is coming home late tonight I'm vegging out here. Besides, the owner of Perk Me Up!, Marla, is super cool. She always piles the whipped cream on my hot chocolate extra high.

Did you know whipped cream has little or no carbs? It's true. You could spray a whole can of whipped cream into your mouth all in one sitting and still have less carbs in your system than one nutritious apple. Nothing compares with extra whipped cream, unless it's a spicy tuna roll from my fave sushi restaurant, Hanabi. Okay, so I admit sushi rolls surrounded by rice aren't exactly lacking in the carb intake department. Sushi rolls are my obsession and addiction, so I give them a wide berth when it comes to counting sushi as high in carb content.

"Your dad working late again?" Marla asks as she wipes off the table next to mine.

I close my algebra book. "Yep. I swear, it's as if the world will collapse if he misses one day."

"He's a dedicated man," Marla says, a newspaper in her hand from someone who left it on a table. "It's admirable."

"I guess."

New customers walk in the door. Marla heads to the register, leaving the newspaper on my table. I notice it's open to the personals. Men seeking women. Women seeking men.

Man, how desperate are people? I mean, who would actually need to go out and advertise for a date?

"What are you doing?" a familiar voice says.

I look up at my best friend, Jessica. She's got dark hair and dark eyes, just like her parents. And her brother and sister. And her cousins. They all look like dark-haired, dark-eyed clones of each other. I swear there's not one recessive gene in her entire Jewish family tree.

"Me? I'm not doing anything." I say, then shove the paper in my backpack.

"Amy," Jess says. "I saw you reading the personals."

"Okay, you caught me." I show her the paper. "Get a load of these ads, Jess. They're so…personal." I feel like I'm *peeping tomming* into these people's lives.

Jess leans in and we both read:

> *Big-Hearted Taurus*
> *SWF, 38, 5'10", lazy but likes music, dancing,*
> *casinos, dining out. Seeking SWM, 30-42, who*
> *likes lazy women for LTR.*

"She can't be serious," I say.

Jess snickers. "Who'd want a lazy gambler?"

We lean our heads together and read more:

> *Professional Model*
> *Sexy SWF, 28, 5'4", 110 lbs., blonde hair, blue*
> *eyes, enjoys trying new things and having fun.*
> *Seeking SWM, 25-65, for LTR.*

Seriously, I'm confused. "Can you please tell me what an LTR is?"

"Long-term telationship."

Oh. I guess I don't have the personals lingo down pat. "Why would a skinny blonde model want a sixty-five-year-old?" I could understand the lazy chick, but the model?

I call Marla over to our table.

"Need more whipped cream, honey?"

"No, thanks," I say. "Why would a model advertise for an LTR in the paper?"

"Huh?"

Jess shakes her head. "Long-term relationship." She holds out the paper to Marla.

"Don't knock it," Marla says. "I know plenty of people who've met their soul mate online or in the personals section."

Jess takes a sip of my hot chocolate. "Amy can't understand. Avi is the perfect guy, right?"

I smile at the mention of my non-boyfriend, who is serving in the Israeli army. We can't really be boyfriend and girlfriend with him a billion miles away. And he's not perfect. A perfect boyfriend wouldn't be living in another country. "What about Mitch?" I ask Jess. "Last week you told me God made him just for you."

She makes a yuck face. "Don't even mention his name around me."

This doesn't sound promising. "All right, what's up?"

Jess sighs. "Well, he hasn't called in two days and the Valentine's Dance is right around the corner. You'd think if he was going to ask me he'd have done it already. My mom wants to go dress shopping but I don't even have a date." She's about to cry. "And I checked my smile in the mirror this morning and realized my face is crooked."

"It is not."

"Is too. See," she says, smiling like she's in pain. "The right side of my mouth droops down."

"Let's go to the dog park," I say, heading off a huge rampage about how bad Mitch is and how crooked her face is. Does she really think God can make everyone totally symmetrical…I mean, give the Big Guy upstairs a break. Besides, Jess has been a hypochondriac and hypercritical of herself ever since third grade when she thought she had lice but it was just bad hair spray flaking. She just needs to chill and redirect her energy into positive thoughts. "I need to walk Mutt."

Mutt's my dog. And yes, he's a mutt. Avi gave Mutt to me before I left Israel. No purebred anything in his blood. He used to be a little fur ball, but in the past two months he's tripled in size.

Back at our condo I fetch my dog and the poop bags. Jess and her one-one-hundredth-of-an-inch crooked face is waiting for me when I walk back outside.

"Oh my God, he's even bigger than when I last saw him," she says, each breath causing puffs of steam in the winter cold.

"I know. If he grows any more I'll have to buy a king-size bed just to fit the both of us," I say, bundling my North Face jacket around me. Visitors here wonder why we Chicagoans brave the cold weather when we could be wearing shorts right now if we lived in Arizona. I'll admit Chicago winters suck if you hate cold weather. I love the cold, I love Chicago, and I love the change in seasons. I need to live in a place where in autumn the leaves actually fall off the trees.

Jessica bites her bottom lip. "You don't think Mitch'll be at the dog park with Zeus, do you?"

Yes. "No. Jess, why don't you just ask him to the dance?"

"So I can be the loser chick of the entire school?"

A bit of an exaggeration, dont'cha think? But I don't disagree with her. Sometimes you challenge Jess, and other times you don't. This would be one of those other times.

Besides, Mitch probably hasn't even thought about the Valentine's Day dance. It's January and the dance isn't until the middle of next month. Guys are a different breed, I tell you. I glance at Jessica, who has this pathetic, sad look on her face.

We're walking down the street with my white, furry monstrosity practically pulling my arm out of my socket. Mutt gets über-excited just going out for a walk. But when he realizes we're going to the dog park, watch out. He's a total spaz about the dog park.

"Can't you send him to doggy boot camp or something?" Jess says as she tries to catch up with us.

"He just came to this country five months ago," I argue. "And he had to be quarantined. I refuse to put him in another stressful situation, the poor guy will need therapy."

Jess shakes her head. "He's a *dog*, Amy. You spoil him way too much."

I do not.

Okay, I do.

But Mutt is my companion. He protects me. He makes me laugh. He's everything to me.

We arrive at the dog park and Mutt can't contain himself. As soon as I close the gate and unlatch the leash from his collar, he romps toward his dog buddies to play.

Mr. Obermeyer, the grumpy old man from the fourteenth floor of our building, sneers at me. "Keep that dog of yours away from Princess."

Princess is Mr. Obermeyer's champion poodle. He hates Mutt. That's just fine because I hate poodles named Princess.

"Don't worry, Mr. Obermeyer," I say. Why the old

man even hangs out at the park is beyond me. He doesn't talk to anyone, except to balk and tell people to keep their dogs away from his pampered pooch.

"Look, there's Mitch!" Jess whispers, then hides behind me.

I look over at the other end of the park and see Mitch. "Let's go talk to him."

"No! Amy, you knew he was gonna be here. Admit it."

It gets to be a problem when people call you out on your passive-aggressive behavior.

"Jess, he's your boyfriend." Okay, Mitch used to be my boyfriend, but that's another story. I'm not into him at all. Besides, I'm content with my non-boyfriend. Well, sort of. I hate the "non" part of it. I wish Avi didn't have me promise not to make any formal commitment to him and vice versa.

Jess peeks over my shoulder. "Don't you see who he's with?"

I crane my neck. A flurry of red hair attached to a long-legged girl comes into view.

Roxanne Jeffries.

I hate Roxanne Jeffries almost as much as I hate dogs named Princess.

She's smiling at Mitch. The *ho.* "Jess, get your ass over there," I order, then move out of the way.

"He's smiling at her! Roxanne doesn't have crooked features, just a crooked personality. Do you think he asked her to the Valentine's Dance?"

"No," I say. "He's *your* boyfriend. What's making you

all insecure? You've got gorgeous straight hair I'd die for, perfect features, and perky boobs. Now go over there and claim your man."

There's no way we can stay undetected. Mutt is the biggest, fluffiest, friendliest dog in the place. In fact, everyone in the neighborhood knows Mutt. And everyone in the neighborhood knows Mutt is my dog. Mitch, who thinks he's too cool to wear a jacket in twenty-five-degree weather, has already spotted my beast and waves to me.

"He sees me," I tell Jess.

"Shit," Jess mutters into my back.

Okay, I've had enough. "He can't ask you if you don't talk to him." I start walking over to Mitch, assuming Jess will follow. "Hi," I say to Mitch and Roxanne. Only now I look back and realize Jess hasn't followed.

Mitch gives me a half wave. "Hey, Amy."

Roxanne, bundled up with a scarf, leather gloves, and a new winter coat I heard she got at Barney's and cost over five hundred dollars, doesn't greet me with a hey, hello, or even a hi. Instead she says, "Your dog is humping Zeus."

I look over at Mutt. She wasn't kidding; he's humping Mitch's black lab like there's no tomorrow. "He's showing Zeus who's the alpha male," I say matter-of-factly.

Roxanne gives Mitch a disgusted look. Mitch laughs.

Mutt hops off Zeus, then takes a huge, steaming dump. Seriously, before I had a dog I would never have thought I'd be okay picking up raunchy, hot steaming dog poop with a plastic bag being the only thing separating me and the excrement.

"Where's Jess going?" Mitch asks.

I quickly scan the dog park and catch sight of Jessica's retreating back. She's leaving. "Come on, Mutt!" I order, then run toward the gate. Mutt is preoccupied with sniffing a pug's butt. Damn. I open the gate, say, "Mutt, treat!" and he comes faster than a horse at the Kentucky Derby.

I have the warm poop bag in one hand and Mutt's leash in the other. The problem is that, instead of stopping so I can put on his leash and dump the poop, Mutt flies right past me, through the open gate, and onto the crowded Chicago street.

"Mutt, get back here!" I yell at the top of my lungs. I swear, when I catch the beast, he's toast.

You'd think my dear dog would listen to me. But no. He's bolting so fast I imagine him singing "Born Free" like I heard on one of those animal shows.

I run about two city blocks which, I might add, are way bigger than any suburban blocks. And my boobs are flapping together, which is not a pretty sight no matter what your gender is. I'm panting and it feels like my lungs are running out of air and shriveling up. I still see a blur of white puffy fur and a wagging tail, but it's getting farther and farther away.

I give a little curse to the snow that melted and is now frozen ice on the sidewalks. I'm slipping and sliding in my boots, which I picked out for fashion and not traction, while trying to avoid the barricades in front of most buildings. If you live or work in Chicago, you know it's a hazard just walking down the streets in winter when ice melts off the tops of the skyscrapers. Ice falls to the street and the people below are targets. Once I got tagged by a chunk of ice from a building. Luckily, I put my head down so I only had a huge lump and serious bruise on top of my head. If I was looking up…well, let's just say I would have either died or my nose would have been broken. I'm careful to look straight ahead and ignore the sounds or warnings of falling ice.

"Mutt!" I scream, but in my state of decreased lung capacity it comes out as a squeak.

I'm about to give up when I see Mutt halt. Thank the Lord. I slide up to the person who stopped him.

A teenager, wearing a geeky button-down plaid shirt and corduroys, is kneeling down and holding Mutt's collar. "Is he yours?" he asks while pushing his glasses high up on his nose as I come to a halt.

I'm huffing and puffing, but I manage a yeah.

Before I can catch my breath and formally thank the guy, he stands up and says, "He should be on a leash, you know. It's the law."

"Thanks for the tip," I say between puffs, then reach out and clip Mutt's leash on.

"Seriously," he says. "He could have been hit by a car."

"Seriously," I say. "I know."

The guy steps toward me. "Do you realize how many dogs are hit by cars or end up in shelters because of careless owners?"

Is this dude kidding me? The last thing I need is a lecture on dog safety. I wave the poop bag, which is still in my hand, at the guy. "Listen, I am not a careless owner. Careless owners do not carry poop bags. And, as you can see, my dog is safe and sound."

He holds his hands up in mock surrender. "Don't get all angry with me. I'm just a concerned citizen."

"Whatever. Thanks for catching my dog," I say, then walk toward home with the poop bag still in my hand.

"Arg!" Mutt barks as we walk.

I look down at my dog and give him my famous sneer, the one where my lip curls up just the right amount. "You are in *so* much trouble."

My dog farts in response. It's a steaming one, too. Yuck.

Talk about passive-aggressive.

2

> *God talked to Moses (Exodus 3:4).*
> *Does God still talk to people?*
> *And how come when I talk to God,*
> *he never seems to answer back?*

On Sunday I drive to Mom's new house in Deerfield with Mutt. Since I moved in with my dad, I visit her on the weekends. Mutt springs inside the house before I even open the door all the way.

"Arg! Arg!"

I don't need to guess where Mom is. Her little shriek alerts me she's in her kitchen. "Amy!"

Here she goes. "What?" I say extremely unenthusiastically.

"Did you have to bring the mutt?"

"Mutt, Mom. His name is Mutt." Okay, so he's also technically a mutt.

"Arg!" Mutt responds.

"Why does he bark like that?"

"I already told you, he's got a speech impediment." It runs in the family. My dad can't say the "th" sound because Israelis don't have the "th" sound in their language. I'm used to it, though, and I don't even hear his accent. It's the same way with Mutt.

"Maybe he's got something wrong with him," she says, backing up. "Did he get all his shots?"

I roll my eyes. "And you call me the drama queen. He's perfectly healthy."

"Just…let him outside, okay? Marc is allergic."

I feel bad leaving Mutt in the cold, especially because I got him in Israel and he's used to the heat. But, hey, he's got a fur coat on so I shouldn't worry. Right?

"Mutt. Out," I order while I open the back door. He doesn't seem to mind going outside, actually, and bounds out the door.

To be honest, I think Marc is allergic to the *idea* of having a dog around. He's a clean freak. And Mutt is a slobbering, shedding animal.

I turn around and find my mom staring at my chest.

"They're looking a little saggy lately. I think it's time to go buy you new bras."

"Mom," I say, horrified. "My bras are fine."

"When was the last time you were fitted properly?"

Oh, no, here we go again. As if I'm going to stand inside a dressing room and have a lady come in, size me up, and watch/help me shove my boobs into bras. Once my mom made me go to one of those specialty bra boutiques.

It was the most embarrassing moment of my life. (Okay, so I've had a ton of embarrassing moments in my life, but that one is high on the list.)

"Can we not talk about my boobs, please?"

Great. Now O Holy Allergic One is walking into the kitchen. I hope he didn't hear the convo about my saggy boobs. "Hi, Amy," he says.

I mumble a "hi."

He leans over my mom and kisses her. Eww! Seriously, if he starts making out with her I'm outta here.

"Ah-choo!"

"Oh, sweetie," Mom says (not referring to me). "Amy's dog was in the house."

"It's okay," he says.

Kiss-ass.

I can't stand all this lovey-dovey stuff. "I'm taking Mutt for a walk."

"Wait. We want to ask you something."

I turn to Mom. "What?"

"Just…come sit down."

I plop down in a chair in the kitchen. Mom sits down beside me. Marc sits next to Mom. She reaches out to hold my hand.

Okay, this is bigger than boob talk. I can tell just by the way Mom is squeezing my hand.

"How would you like to be a big sister?"

I shrug. "I wouldn't."

I like my life just how it is. I have my mom, I have my dad, I have Jessica, I have my non-boyfriend Avi, and

I have Mutt. My life is fine, why would I want a little brat screwing it up?

Mom's excitement deflates.

"Why, were you thinking about adopting a baby? Listen, Mom, I doubt people would even allow you adopt at your age."

"I beg your pardon. I'm only thirty-seven."

Duh! "You're almost forty!"

"Besides," she says, ignoring me. "We're not thinking of adopting. I'm pregnant."

Pause.

Silence.

Back up. Did I hear right?

"You're *pregnant*? As in you're going to have a baby *pregnant*?"

Marc smiles wide. "Yep."

I stand up. "And you didn't consult me on this?" I mean, you'd think they would have at least talked to me about it. Are they replacing me because I moved in with my dad? It's not like I don't come around the 'burbs. I do. But Mom just up and sold our condo in the city. I couldn't move schools my junior year. Then I would have to make all new friends. Oh, man. And they're so excited about it, too. Like the new, shiny kid is going to be way better than the old, used model.

A baby.

There's no getting around the fact that I'm being replaced.

"I'm not changing diapers," I blurt out. Yes, I know

it was immature and childish to say that, but it just came out. Sue me for being a teenager.

Mom gives me a tearful look. "You don't have to change diapers."

I'm sorry, I just can't stand here calmly. My mind is whirling with questions. "Was this planned?"

Marc and Mom look at each other. "Well, yeah," he says.

"And you didn't think it was important to ask my opinion?"

"Amy, Marc and I want to have children together. I thought you'd be as excited as we are."

I swallow, which is no easy feat because I have a lump in my throat the size of a basketball.

"I gotta go," I say, and get Mutt. "Come on, boy," I say, leading him to the front of the yard. I need to get away from the house and figure out where I fit in my so-called family.

My mom runs after me. "Amy, stay. I don't want you to be angry."

I sigh. "I'm not angry, Mom. I just need to sort this all out in my head." In my car, I flip open my phone to text Jessica.

Me: Guess who's pregnant?
Jess: u?
Me: Get real.
Jess: ur mom?
Me: yep

Jess: Mazel tov!?
Me: Don't congratulate me, plz
Jess: Could b worse
Me: How?
Jess: Could b u?
Me: I'm a virgin.
Jess: Nobody's perfect.
Me: Don't make me laugh.
Jess: Better than crying, right?

Leave it to my best friend to put it into perspective. But Jessica doesn't know that there's history with my mom and dad. History that I think still stings for one of my parents. And that is no laughing matter.

When I get back to the city, I swear the temperature in the city has decreased by at least twenty degrees. It mimics the chill in my body.

Crying isn't my thing, but my eyes water on their own. Damn.

I feel sorry for my dad, even more now that I know Mom and Marc are really going to have a new family. My poor dad is alone. He'll never get my mom back now. When he finds out about the baby, he's really going to get depressed. I'll have to do something about that, sooner rather than later. My perfect family life just blew up in my face.

Are families supposed to drive you crazy? I need to talk to someone about this. I'd like to talk to my non-boyfriend, but he's somewhere in the middle of Israel in training. No phone calls during boot camp.

I glance at the picture of Avi on my nightstand. He's in his army fatigues, a machine gun strapped to his shoulder. And he's smiling. Smiling. As if being stuck in the middle of the hot Negev Desert during military boot camp is no biggie. I miss him more than anything right now. He's so strong, inside and out. I wish I was like that.

In his last letter he wrote about stars. He said in the Negev Desert at night he looked up and the sky was so clear he could swear he saw a billion stars.

He said he thought of me right there, wondering what I was doing under the same stars. My heart just about melted into garlic butter sauce (which I love to dip my pizza in) when I read his letter. Sometimes I feel like he has the right perspective on life. Me? I'd probably look up at billions of stars and think, *I'm so insignificant.*

I sit on my bed and open my backpack. There, staring back at me, is the personals section. I must have shoved it in there accidentally. I wipe my eyes and focus on the paper.

A small idea, as tiny as a faraway star, starts forming in the back of my mind.

If Mom and Marc can create their own little suburban family, I'm going to create one of my own for my bachelor dad…right here in the city.

After all, what's wrong with placing a personal ad for my dad? Maybe, as Marla said, he could meet his own soul mate.

3

Kosher question # 1: In Leviticus (11:1), God lists what's kosher and what's not. Nowhere in the entire Bible does it mention anything about spicy tuna sushi rolls with little pieces of tempura crunch inside.

Hunky, brooding single Jewish dad with an adorable teenage daughter seeks woman for dinners, dancing, and walks in the park. Needs to like dogs and be free of any neurosis or hang-ups.

"Amy, I'm home. And I brought sushi for you."

I shove the draft into my backpack and rush for the door. Okay, okay, I know the ad needs a little tweaking. But I'll deal with that later. Sushi can't wait. "Did you get spicy tuna rolls?"

"Yes."

I kiss him on the cheek and say, "You're the best. Did you remember to ask for tempura flakes inside?"

"Sorry, I forgot. I hope they're still edible."

He's joking with me because he's well aware I'll devour the spicy tuna rolls with or without the tempura crunch.

My dad is sifting through the mail by the front door. He lives for mail. Sundays he positively goes nuts not having any. When Monday rolls around, he's like a hawk.

I snatch the white takeout bag off the table by the front door. My mouth is already watering in anticipation of eating freshly made sushi. "How was work?"

"Hectic as usual. How was school?"

"Hectic as usual."

He looks sideways at me.

"Well, it was," I say. "I had three tests, one I probably failed, two hours of homework, and I have no date for the Valentine's Dance. Top that."

We walk into the kitchen together. "Avi is in Israel," he says as if I'm pining for a relationship that's bound to fail. Talk about the "like father, like daughter" syndrome.

"I know," I say.

My dad gives me a weak smile and shrugs. "I just don't want you to miss out."

Mutt bounds into the kitchen and starts jumping on me. "Arg!"

"We have to get him fixed," he says.

I sit on the kitchen floor with Mutt and pat his springy hair. "We aren't going to do that," I tell my dog. "Only mean people do that to their dogs."

Mutt responds by licking my face. There's no way I'm having my dog's balls cut off.

My dad takes extra food for himself out of the refrigerator because he mistakingly treats sushi as an appetizer. He says sushi doesn't fill him up. "Amy…"

I give him my I-am-not-backing-down stare. "What?"

"The vet said—"

"Yeah, and the vet thought Mutt was a goldendoodle, too. Can you believe that? A *designer* mutt, no less. I don't trust that guy." Give me a break. My dog is a pure, un-poodleized mutt.

My dad takes a piece of pita and swipes it into a container of hummus. It's his staple food. Israelis are to hummus as frat boys are to beer. (We've been studying analogies in English. Can you tell?)

"Don't double dip," I warn him.

"I wouldn't dream of it," he says, stuffing the pita into his mouth.

"Maybe you haven't had a date in a while because you shove food into your mouth when you eat," I say.

"Maybe I haven't had a date in a while because I've been busy," he says back.

Yeah, right. "So what kind of woman do you like?"

"Why?"

"Maybe I can help you."

"Amy, we are not having this discussion."

"But—"

"But nothing. Stop thinking about finding me a date and start concentrating on your schoolwork."

I assure you schoolwork is a lot more boring. "You know what your problem is?" I ask him.

"Yes. I have a daughter who insists she knows everything."

"That's not your problem, *Aba*. That's your blessing."

My dad chuckles, then sets our dinner on the table.

Taking the chopsticks from the takeout bag, I pick up a spicy tuna roll from the platter and dip it into a little container of soy sauce. I'm so glad he got sushi from my favorite place. They always have the tuna without any stringy white veins attached. I do not eat sushi with stringy white veins attached. After I pop the roll into my mouth, my insides smile.

"I forgot to ask," my dad says. "How was it at your mom's yesterday?"

I gauge his reaction as I say, "She's pregnant."

The poor man puts down his fork and stares at me. "Really?"

I nod. I can't talk now even if I wanted to. I refuse to get emotional.

"Wow."

He goes back to eating after his "wow" comment. I want to apologize even though it's not my fault. He's probably devastated my mom chose a dork over him. Now she's not only married to the new guy, but she's had sex with him to procreate. Eww. The thought of my mom having sex at her age is just plain gross. The fact that she's having it with my stepdad is even grosser.

The only way to fix this situation is to find my dad a wife. Not for procreation, but so he doesn't feel like the odd one without a partner. He's for sure hiding his true feelings, covering up his devastation of losing my mom to make me feel better.

After we finish dinner, he goes to the workout room in the building while I make a beeline for the computer.

I'm web surfing. Don't worry, I know not to give out any personal information when I'm in chat rooms. My dad is a consultant for the Department of Homeland Security and has bored me to death with the dangers of the Internet until I thought my ears would bleed.

I'm not interested in chat rooms, no siree bob. I'm focused purely on finding my dad a wife. Now…where can I find the perfect woman?

I surf the Net until I finally find it. Yeah!

Professional Jewish Singles Network.

They guarantee *you will find the Jewish mate a matchmaker would be jealous of.*

I saw *Fiddler on the Roof.* This is the best possible news.

My heart races as I read the home page and the requirements to join the PJSN. Need to be single. Duh! Need to be between the ages of twenty-one and seventy-five. Check. My dad is a whopping thirty-seven. Need to have a college degree. Check. My dad has a degree from the University of Illinois. Need to have a credit card to pay the $59.99 monthly fee.

Okay, the credit card thing is going to take a little manipulation.

My eyes dart over to the front door. His wallet is on

the table where we put the mail. I know his credit card is inside.

I saunter over to his wallet. I've used my mom's credit card before. Of course I had permission then.

It wouldn't hurt just to take the card out. Just to look at it. I slowly open his wallet. Yep, in one slot the top of a shiny gold credit card is staring back at me. I slip it out and glance nervously at the front door.

I have at least thirty minutes before he comes back. After I put the wallet back on the table I trot back to the computer with his credit card in my hand. I'm not thinking about how it's probably illegal that I'm using someone else's card—this is about helping my father.

The words in my head are chanting *soul mate, soul mate, soul mate.* My dad can't just live the rest of his life in solitary misery.

I click the word *Register.* The computer prompts me to answer a list of questions. My fingers automatically type in the info.

Name: Ron Barak
Age: 37
Hair color: dark brown
Eye color: dark brown
Children: one *delightful* seventeen-year-old
Occupation: security consultant
State: Illinois
Hobbies: reading, hiking, tennis, baseball

Okay, I'm having a tough time with the hobbies question. And, to be completely honest, I've fudged a few of the hobbies I listed. My dad doesn't know the first thing about baseball. It's not exactly a popular Israeli sport. But if you live in Chicago, you gotta be into either baseball, basketball, hockey, or football. This is a sport-centered town. I'm not even going to get into the Cubs/Sox, North Side/South Side rivalry.

On to the next question: *Describe yourself in two words.*

Hmm…what two words will attract women? I type in *Israeli* and *hunk* something quick and click *enter*. It prompts me to scan a picture for his profile and I find one from our trip to Israel.

Finally, it asks for my credit card number. I mean *his* credit card number. I punch in the numbers and before you can say "stolen credit card," my dad has his own profile, PJSN e-mail, and is ready to meet his soul mate. Oh man, oh man, I am excited. My dad is in the Professional Jewish Singles Network and is ready to join the dating scene.

Oh, shit. I hear the door opening and I still have my dad's credit card in my hot little hand. *Do something quick,* my mind tells me.

I slide the credit card under the keyboard and close all of the open windows on the computer. I'll place the Visa back in his wallet later. By the time he figures out I used it, he'll be so thrilled to have met his future wife he won't get pissed off. In fact, he'll be thanking me all the way to the rabbi who'll marry them.

"Amy?"

He's onto me. He knows I took his credit card without permission. Oh, no. I swallow, hard. "Yeah?"

"Don't you think Mutt needs to go out?"

I let out a breath. "Uh, I guess."

"Well…"

I stand up, put the leash on Mutt, and dash to the elevator. As soon as the elevator door opens, I'm pushed back by a huge cardboard box and almost fall backwards. My boobs are squished, I tell you. I probably just went from a saggy C+ cup to an A– cup.

"Hey!" I yell.

"Sorry," a masculine voice murmurs, then the guy puts down the box.

But he's not a man, at least not a real one. It's the boy from yesterday who caught Mutt and gave me the *concerned citizen* lecture.

Today he's wearing a green plaid shirt and jeans with a waist way too high. And I swear cranky Mr. Obermeyer has those same gym shoes.

"Arg!" Mutt barks, then tries to sniff his crotch as if he's hiding a treat in there.

Concerned Citizen covers his privates with his hands like a soccer player during a penalty kick. Then he pushes his glasses high up on his nose, the rims circling his green eyes. "Oh, it's you."

I pull Mutt away from his pants. "Just watch where you're going next time. As a *concerned citizen*," I add, "you should know not to crash into people with large boxes."

With my rant I miss the elevator. Damn. I push the down arrow again.

He steps forward and trips over the box. "Are you always this friendly?"

I don't even answer him. Where does he come off challenging me? Thankfully the elevator dings and the door opens. I hurry inside with Mutt. There's no way I'm missing my second chance at freedom.

"Arg!"

As the elevator door closes, he bends over to pick up the box again. I wonder what this boy is doing in my building, on my floor, in my life.

Avi says everything happens for a reason. I hate to disagree, but he's wrong.

4

I've seen **Fiddler on the Roof.** *There was this one lady,*
Yente, who was the matchmaker—that was her job in the
village. Right now I'm the matchmaker.
Maybe I've found my calling…

"Hey, girl," Marla says as I walk into Perk Me Up! after
school the next day. "Jessica is at the computer corner."

Marla said she put in the computers because people
wanted to be connected to the Internet and their e-mail no
matter where they are. And if they want free, convenient
Internet while they're drinking her coffee, all the better.

I stand behind Jessica. "What are you doing?"

Her hands are busy clicking away. "Checking Mitch's
e-mail."

"Sneaky, Jess. How'd you get his password?"

"I have my ways. See, that bitch Roxanne is e-mailing
him," Jess says, pointing to the screen.

Oooh, gossip. I know it's bad, but gossip is seriously addictive and underrated. "What does she say?"

"Just that she needs help in biology, yadda yadda."

"You better watch out for her," I say. "Now get off the computer so I can check something."

"I'm still mad at you, you know."

Me? Innocent, little me? "You'll get over it. Besides, whatever I did was probably for your own good."

"You took me to the dog park knowing Mitch would be there. Stop meddling in my life."

I huff. "I'm Jewish, what do you expect? I was born to meddle."

Jessica shakes her head. Okay, so she has more Jewish blood because both her parents are Jewish and my dad is the one who gave me my Jewish genes. My mom gave me good fashion sense genes.

While Jessica goes to the bathroom, I quickly check the PJSN website and log into my father's profile.

Oh. My. God.

I've got thirty-seven responses from women who want to date me…I mean, my dad. And, checking the home page, my dad has gotten the most hits on the PJSN website in the past twenty-four hours.

It brings popularity to a whole new level.

I'm almost giddy (does anyone use that word anymore??) as I scan the responses of women.

Three make sexual innuendos. They're out.

Ten live in the suburbs. Definitely out.

Five don't put their pictures on the site. Questionable. What if the supposed woman is a man?

Seven are over fifty. Ten have more than two kids. Out. Out. My dad can hardly handle me. How would he be able to handle a whole tribe?

That leaves two.

One is in human resources, the other a lawyer. I e-mail both of them and ask them if they want to have coffee sometime. Okay, it's a little creepy asking women out on dates. But even more daunting is having to manipulate my dad somehow to get him to go on the date. I know meeting for coffee isn't the most original date, but at least it's not a dinner or lunch where you have to sit and talk the entire time, waiting for that uncomfortable silence when you both want to escape.

"Does your dad know about this?"

I shriek and scold Jessica. "Didn't your mother tell you it's not nice to sneak up on people?"

"No."

My best friend shakes her head and puts her hand over her eyes. "Please tell me you didn't sign your dad up for an online dating service."

"I didn't sign my dad up for an online dating service."

"You're lying, Amy."

"Of course I'm lying."

"Amy, one of these days your little plans are gonna backfire and come crashing in your face."

"Oh, ye of little faith," I say. "My dad will have a girl-friend by Passover."

"Oh, ye of too many scatterbrained ideas," Jess says. "Your head is getting bigger than your boobs."

"Shut up. Haven't you ever needed something you didn't want?"

"Yeah, a flu shot. And it hurt me way more than it hurt my mom who made me get one."

Jessica doesn't understand. "You don't expect me to sit around as my mom makes babies with Marc while my dad stays alone for the rest of his life, do you?" It makes me sad thinking he's pining for my mom.

"Your dad doesn't seem to mind," Jess says.

I turn in my chair and face her. I admit my dad doesn't outwardly show his unhappiness, but it's in there. Deep down. And he's starting to age. "He's got a few gray hairs already."

"Your parents are way younger than mine, Amy. My dad is totally bald and my mom's almost fifty and is totally white . . . well, underneath all of the hair dye she's as white as a snowball."

"Great. In a few years my mom'll turn gray and people will think my little sister or brother is my own kid. They'll think my mom is the grandma."

"People in their late thirties have babies all the time. Don't stress about it."

I put my hands over my heart. "Me, stress? I never stress about anything."

Jess raises her eyebrows at me and chuckles. Because we both know it's not true.

My cell phone is ringing. I click the little green button. It's my dad. "Hey, *Aba*."

"Amy, I just took my clients out for dinner. I'm about to pay the bill."

"So?"

"So," he says in a distressed voice. "Do you by any chance know where my credit card is?"

Oh, no. I forgot to put it back in his wallet after my run-in with Geek Boy. "Umm...*Aba*...you're not gonna believe this—"

5

To make a sin offering to God:
a) sacrifice an animal to the Lord (Leviticus 6:18) or
b) wait until Yom Kippur and fast a whole day.
(Leviticus 16:29)
So good to know I can erase my sins.
(Erasing guilt is outlined in Leviticus 5.
If God can forgive, surely humans should, too.)

I'm grounded for the rest of my life.

My dad laid down that law a few minutes ago, and he sounded dead serious. Now I hear his little outbursts of anger coming from the kitchen.

The phone rings. It's probably Jessica.

"Don't you *dare* pick dat phone up!" he yells from the other end of the condo, his thick Hebrew accent getting thicker by the minute. I swear, the neighbors are going to start calling the police soon if he doesn't calm down.

I hear him stomping closer to my room. He opens the door and scowls at me while running a hand through his hair, his signature and patented I-am-frustrated-and-don't-know-what-to-do-with-my-teenage-daughter move. "Do you not understand what you did was wrong on so many levels, Amy? You stole my credit card—"

"Borrowed it," I correct him.

"You made me look like a fool in front of clients. You sign me up for a dating service…what's next?"

Before I can open my mouth to defend myself, he says, "How much did it cost me?"

"The dating service?"

He nods.

"Um…less than sixty dollars a month," I answer.

"How much less?"

"One penny."

"Go on the computer now and cancel it before I have to pay for two months."

"Um, *Aba*?"

"What?"

"I got you a six-month subscription. It was cheaper to pay it all up front. I got a deal. Think of me as your Yente from *Fiddler on the Roof*. Your personal matchmaker."

This time he laughs, and I think he's broken way past the anger barrier and is quickly gliding toward delirium. A delirious Israeli ex-commando is not a good thing.

"What's the problem with a dating service? It's for *Jews*," I interject, hoping to lessen the blow. "You gotta love Jewish women. You're Israeli."

"That's not the point. You used my credit card without asking."

"Yeah, well, I don't exactly have one of my own."

I swear I hear him praising that fact under his breath.

The doorbell rings. Mutt is going nuts, barking non-stop. "Arg! Arg! Arg! Arg!" It gets my dad's attention. He's afraid he'll have to pay a fine if we get too many complaints from the neighbors about Mutt's excessive barking. I'm saved from my dad's rant for now. *Thank you, Mutt!*

"Stay here," my dad orders, leaving my room.

So now I'm sitting on my bed, alone once again. And I'm grounded. I wonder how long I'll be stuck here before he gives in.

"Amy, come here!" he calls out.

"Yeah?" I say innocently as I head to the foyer of our condo. Dad is holding Mutt's collar, holding him back from jumping on and sniffing the crotch of whoever is at the door. I've had the talk with Mutt, but he doesn't listen. I don't know what the big deal about crotches is. I assume once you've smelled one, you've smelled them all. Not that I'd know. I have no desire to go near anyone else's to test my theory.

"You know Mrs. Keener, don't you?"

I scan the suit and tailored attire of the woman, sure she hasn't smiled in at least a year. Can she pull that 1970s bun tighter on her skull? I turn my gaze to the person beside her. Oh, no. It's Concerned Citizen Boy, in the flesh.

Mrs. Keener pushes him closer to us and directs her conversation to my dad. "This is my nephew, Nathan. He's come to live with us for a while." She shakes her head as she says, "It's a long story. I know your daughter is about the same age and was wondering if she'd be able to show him around the city."

Nathan looks about as happy as I do to be in this situation. But I suppose being grounded and stuck in my room is worse than being stuck with Nathan Keener.

Nathan Keener.

Just the name alone could get a kid beat up.

"Amy's grounded," my dad says.

Thanks a lot for sharing that humiliating piece of information, Dad.

"Oh," Mrs. Keener says, obviously put in an awkward situation.

"But I guess if she takes Mutt for a walk, she could go out for a bit—"

Needing no further push, I grab Mutt's leash off our hall tree and snap it on his collar. "Come on, Nathan," I call over my shoulder as I hurry to the elevator with a very excited and very large puppy.

Nathan, it seems, needs no further push either. He follows right behind me and enters the elevator as soon as Mutt and I step inside.

We have no elevator music in our building, so it's just silence except for heavy panting courtesy of my dog.

"You don't have to babysit me, you know," he says while crossing his arms over his chest, trying to look tough. He doesn't.

"Your aunt seems to think I do," I reply.

The elevator door opens. Nathan Keener is right behind me, not missing a step when I exit our building. But once I turn toward the dog park, I don't hear his footsteps behind me anymore. Turning around, I find Nathan walking in the opposite direction. With his long, corduroy-wrapped legs, he's already half a block away.

Mutt is pulling me toward the park. "Hey, Nathan!" I yell, but the guy doesn't turn around. Now what am I supposed to do?

6

Chicken soup can help heal you
when you're sick. Is there a recipe for healing
relationships?

If you can believe it, I found out this morning Nathan Keener is going to my school, a private prep school called Chicago Academy. Yep, it's true. I also have the pleasure of sitting behind him in English class and he's even in gym class with me. It wouldn't be so bad, but he's already the talk of the entire school.

What is it about transfer students that fascinates people so much? If I hear one more time, *Amy, did you see the new guy?* I swear I'm gonna scream. It's fifth period. I have study hall. I sit next to Kyle Sanderson, the varsity center for Chicago Academy's basketball team and all-around popular guy. The only flaw is that Kyle wears no less than a half a bottle of cologne every day. You can tell when Kyle leaves a classroom that he's been there. He's like a bear, leaving his scent behind for girls.

"What's up, Nelson?" he says, calling me by my last name as he slides skillfully into the seat next to me. Do you think he practices that move?

I'm not about to tell him I've been hyphenating my last name since the beginning of the school year, using both my parents' last names. I'm now Amy Nelson-Barak. I'm not telling Kyle because 1) he wouldn't care and 2) he wouldn't remember even if I did tell him.

"Not much," I respond.

"That's not what I heard."

Huh?

"What'd you hear?" I ask him. Is there a rumor about me?

"That you signed up for a dating service."

"Who told you that?" It's not true…exactly.

Kyle leans his chair back on two legs. "The new guy. You know, the one with glasses and dorky clothes."

"Nathan?"

Kyle shrugs his big shoulders and says, "Yep. The dude's my bio partner this week."

I'm going to kill that tall, lanky jerk who wouldn't know the difference between Dana Buchman and Armani. How dare he spread rumors about me!

"So…are you that hard up?" Kyle asks. "'Cause you're kinda cute, Nelson, and you got great boobage."

I whip my head around and glare at him. "Boobage? Jeez, Kyle, do you make these words up?"

He puts his hands up in question. "You'd rather I said tits?"

"Shut up," I say before opening my trig book and sticking my head in it. I swear, if he keeps staring at my chest I'm going to make sure he can't pass the ball at the next basketball game.

"Miss Barak, would you care to share your conversation with the rest of us?" Mr. Hennesey barks out from the front of the room. Mr. Hennesey is the gym teacher as well as study hall monitor. Study hall policeman is more like it.

If Kyle mentions my *boobage* to the rest of the room, I'm going to kill him...along with Nathan Keener.

"Nope," I say.

"Then I suggest you both quit talking or I'll have to separate you." I wish.

Ten minutes later, Mr. Hennesey walks out of the room. As everyone knows, when a teacher walks out of the room it's an invitation to start talking. Right now I don't want to talk.

"You need a date for the Valentine's Dance?" Kyle says, loudly I might add.

I cock my head to the side and answer sweetly, "Why? Are you asking me?" Ha! Right back at ya. Nothing like a lowly junior putting a popular senior boy on the spot.

I'm sure everyone in the entire room hears our conversation. The snickers and looks in our direction are a clue. I think the words "Valentine's Dance" alone would turn heads. It's on everyone's mind since the posters went up last week.

"I will, if you want to do a threesome. I already asked Caroleen Connors, but I'm man enough to take you both on at once."

Kyle has the nerve to wink at me. Eww! The guy needs a serious ego adjustment.

Mr. Hennesey walks back into the room, so I can't respond. So now I'm sitting here, seething at Kyle for being a male chauvinist pig and at Nathan for spreading rumors about me.

After study hall, I walk to social studies while plotting ways to confront the geek who moved into my building. Is he *that* socially inept he has to stoop to spreading rumors about me just to get attention?

"Did you see the new guy?"

I look up at my friend Raine, who has no clue my heart rate just jumped and my veins tensed at the mention of him. I look up at her with my patented sneer.

"What did I do?" Raine asks, wide-eyed.

"Nothing," I say. "Just please don't talk about Nathan Keener."

A guy's voice behind me says, "FYI, it's Nathan Greyson."

I'm left with my mouth wide open, staring at my neighbor and his oversized tortoise-rimmed glasses slipping down the bridge of his nose.

Raine says, "Nice pants," and walks away giggling.

"You and your friends really know how to throw out the welcome mat," Nathan says with a fake smile. "Private schools are a breeding ground for fake, plastic people. This school is no exception."

I don't understand this guy. He's geeky, but he's got

an attitude that doesn't mix with his outward appearance. "Who *are* you?" I ask.

"Hell if I know," he responds, and without another word walks away.

Leaving me to wonder if he's a vampire or alien in human form.

I walk into social studies and the last thing on my mind is current affairs. But Mrs. Moore is obsessed with vibrant class discussions on the president, his policies, and making sure we all know what's going on in this great country of ours. I think the mere act of looking at the American flag brings her to tears.

When the bell rings at the end of the day, I stuff my homework in my book bag and trudge through the slush to the bus stop with Jessica, Cami, and Raine. Mitch is standing at the bus stop already, and when Jessica walks close he casually puts his arm across her shoulders. I can tell Jess is still upset he hasn't asked her to the dance. She's as stiff as the icicles hanging from the bus stop sign.

"Seriously, Amy. Did you join a dating service to get a date for the Valentine's Dance?" Roxanne says, and laughs like a hyena giving painful birth to twins.

I *really* hate her. She knows it, too, because last year we almost came to blows in tennis when I bumped her down from the varsity team to JV. The cheat always pretends to hyperventilate in the middle of a match she's losing so she can take a break and regroup. Nice try, Roxy. I still beat your butt.

"She's got a boyfriend," Jessica chimes in while rolling her eyes. "Leave her alone, Roxanne."

I want to cheer *Go Jessica Go!*, but don't. Jessica doesn't reveal the fact that I signed my dad up on PJSN because she knows it would embarrass me. One of these days Roxanne is going to find herself banned from the bus stop if her mouth keeps running like diarrhea.

Unfortunately, we have to wait ten more minutes for the bus to come. We all live on the Gold Coast and have to take public transportation to school. It doesn't make sense to have a car when you live and go to school in the city. So we're at the mercy of the Chicago Transit Authority. It's cool during the summer and spring, but when snow dumps itself on Chicago it can get pretty rough. We ususally wait inside the school until the last possible minute, then trudge outside and freeze our butts off until the bus stops and opens its doors.

As if standing next to Roxanne wasn't bad enough, Nathan comes sidling up the sidewalk and stands with us. He's got his iPod headphones in his ears, highlighting that he doesn't care to start conversations with fake, plastic people. Kyle kind of nods his head in acknowledgment of him. Nathan nods back, then pushes his glasses up again. Someone should clue him in that they sell non-slip glasses now.

The bus turns down the street. Relief time! I'm the first one on, ready to get out of Roxanne and Nathan's sight even if it's for ten seconds. I head to the back of the bus where we hang until our stop. Jess and Mitch—"the couple"—sit across from me. Cami and Raine sit together, so do Kyle and Roxanne. That leaves Nathan and me, the singles.

Nathan doesn't even contemplate sitting next to me as he and his headphones plop themselves down onto a bench in the front of the bus. He makes it very clear he doesn't consider himself one of us.

I have no clue why this irks me so much.

Maybe it's because he insulted my school and my friends. And me.

Whatever. I don't care what Nathan ~~Keener~~ Greyson thinks about me. I have my own friends and boyfriend, even if he does live halfway around the globe.

Ugh. I miss Avi, especially at times like these when I need someone just to ramble to. Jess has been depressed lately—I have no clue if it's really about Mitch or if something else is bugging her. She won't open up to me.

Cami is studiously doing her homework so she has less to do when she gets home. And Raine is just the opposite, concentrating on putting her lip-gloss on to keep it fresh. She doesn't give a crap about homework. In fact, I bet she probably has her mom do it for her.

Roxanne is flirting with Kyle. Maybe she's moving on to someone who doesn't have a girlfriend. I wonder if she knows he's going to the Valentine's Dance with Caroleen Connors. Probably not by the way she's leaning into him and touching him as if he's her property. I swear, Kyle just eats up the attention. But thank God he's focused on her *boobage* now instead of mine.

The bus stops on the corner of Dearborn and Superior, where I get off. Of course Nathan gets off the bus, too, and we walk into our building together. Elevators are a strange place to begin with. The creaky sounds and rattling of the doors can put anyone on edge. But when you're in the elevator with someone you don't particularly like, the place can make even a non-claustrophobe feel like they're stuck in a coffin.

I'm on one side of the elevator; Nathan is on the other. He still has his iPod earbuds in his ears, but I have no clue if there's music playing in them. I almost want to say something to test him. I know people who pretend they're listening to music but are really eavesdropping on conversations when others think they can't hear.

"I'm not plastic," I say to him. "Or fake."

No reaction, except for a little twitch of his jaw. And his breathing halted, just for a millimeter of a second.

It's true. I'm as real as they get, no holds barred. My dad says sometimes it's a good trait, and sometimes it's a horrible one.

We finally reach the fortieth floor.

"Check ya later, Barbie," Nathan mumbles.

Did I just hear right?

Barbie? Um…that's not gonna fly with me. No way, no how.

I stop dead in my tracks and turn around. "What did you call me?" I ask.

I should have known the guy would ignore me. Ignoring is apparently Nathan's specialty.

Inside my condo, Mutt greets me with a pounce and a germ-infested lick. Most people say that a dog's mouth is cleaner than a person's mouth. But most people haven't tested my dog's mouth. He licks too many private parts to be considered clean by anyone's standards.

I look up when Mutt runs over to his leash. To my surprise, my dad is sitting at the dining room table.

"You get fired?" I ask.

My dad looks up. "No. Just wanted to be here when you got home."

That's a first. "Why?"

My dad's attention is taken by Mutt, holding the leash in his mouth and wagging his tail around like a lance. "Let's talk about it after you take Mutt out."

This doesn't sound too good. "Tell me now."

"He's going to have an accident on the floor if you don't take him."

"I'm going to freak out if you don't tell me. What's worse?"

My dad takes a deep breath and says, "I'm new at being a fadder, but I have to try my best. You used my credit card without my permission. You signed me up for a dating service without my permission. That six-month membership is costing me over three hundred dollars."

That about sums it up. "I said I was sorry."

"This time, Amy, sorry isn't good enough."

Now I'm starting to panic. Does he want me to leave and go live with my mom and her hyper-allergic husband? There's no way they'll let me keep Mutt in their pristine suburban house with the new baby coming. And will I have to start a new school with kids I don't know? High school is tough enough without being the new kid, and I'm not going to think about Nathan right now because he doesn't deserve my sympathy.

"I'll do anything, *Aba*. Please don't send me away."

My dad stands. I can tell he's going to break the bad news right now and I wince. "I'm not going to send you away, sweetheart."

"You're not?"

"No. I got you a job."

7

Moses had incredible negotiation skills. He made God, The
#1 Top Guy, *change his mind about destroying all of the
Jewish people (Exodus 32:13). If that doesn't prove anyone
can change the course of their life, nothing will. I wish I
had Moses's negotiation skills when dealing with my dad.*

"Amy, what are you doing here so early? Conversion class
doesn't start for another ten minutes."

I'm standing in the doorway of Rabbi Glassman's office
at Temple Beit Chaverim. The rabbi is reading over papers
while he rubs his gray and black beard.

"I need to talk to someone," I tell him.

Putting his papers aside, Rabbi Glassman motions for
me to sit at the chair opposite his desk. "I'm always here to
listen if someone needs an ear. That's my job."

"Listening to people complain?"

"Among other things," he says with a smile, then leans
back in his large cushioned chair. "What's on your mind?"

Lots of stuff, but I'm going to pick out the top one bugging me. "I got in trouble."

"With the law?" he prompts.

"With my dad. I took his credit card without his permission and now he wants me to pay him back the money I charged." I look to the rabbi, to make sure he's not keeling over in shock or shame.

"What did you charge, if I may ask?"

I put my hands up. "I know this is gonna sound weird, but it was for a good reason. I signed up for PJSN...you know, the Professional Jewish Singles Network. It's a dating service. And I did it for my dad."

The rabbi's eyebrows raise up. "You signed your father up for a dating service without his permission?"

I nod. "He needs a wife."

Rabbi Glassman sighs, then says in a quiet voice, "Amy, sometimes you have to let people choose their own paths in life."

"Yeah, but what if they're taking the wrong one?"

"Everyone makes mistakes. Even rabbis. We're all human."

I seem to be making more than my share of human mistakes lately. "So you're saying I should let my dad live his life alone and lonely?"

"Nonsense. He has you, doesn't he? Some things aren't measured by their size, but by their importance."

"That's very philosophical, Rabbi," I say, smiling.

"You caught me on a good day."

I bite the inside of my cheek. "I haven't had a lot of those lately."

"Ah, but you can't appreciate a great day unless you've experienced bad ones."

"Like Jonah had when God made the whale eat him?"

"I see you've been studying for class."

I lean forward and whisper, "Yeah, although I don't really buy it all, Rabbi. It's a little far-fetched for me, if you know what I mean. Can I still be a Jew if my brain can't grasp around certain Bible stories?"

The reason I can talk to Rabbi Glassman honestly is because he's never judged me or laughed at my opinions or arguments in class. He makes me feel like everything I have to say is really important and smart. Even when I'm disagreeing with him.

Rabbi Glassman leans forward and whispers back, "Amy, I think it's far-fetched, too."

My mouth goes wide. "You do? Don't worry, Rabbi. Your secret is safe with me."

Rabbi Glassman smiles and says, "I think it all comes down to faith and trust."

"In people?" I ask.

He shrugs, as if he doesn't have all the answers to all of his questions. "In people…in God…in yourself. Do you think you have faith and trust?"

I look up at him. "Should I answer that now?"

My rabbi shakes his head. "I don't know if you're ready to answer that yet. Why don't you think about it for a while and get back to me when you're…let's say…twenty years old."

I stand up, taking in all the information Rabbi Glassman

gave me as I leave his office. "See you at class, Rabbi," I call over my shoulder. "And thanks for the talk."

"Any time," he calls back.

Five minutes later, I'm in conversion class with five other people. Even though my father is Jewish, my mother isn't. I've lived with my mom most of my life, and she raised me without any religion. I went to Israel this past summer and realized I was missing something in my life: being Jewish. So I'm learning as much about my faith as I can.

Hence the conversion class.

We meet once a week. Rabbi Glassman has us read stories from the Bible and we discuss our opinions and reflect on the meaning or lessons behind the stories. He also teaches us about the different Jewish holidays and laws. The rabbi says a lot of Judaism comes from traditions. Since I don't really have any Jewish traditions, I'm going to have to make up some myself.

Back at home, I take Mutt out then walk over to Perk Me Up! Yes, I'm officially a Perk Me Up! employee, thanks to my father and Marla. My punishment is a job at my favorite café, and I'm not thrilled about it.

Marla greets me with a huge smile. "Nice to see we're all perky this evening."

"It's been a long day."

"Oh, then maybe I'll just have you sweep floors and wipe off tables so you don't have to interact with the customers."

I put a fake smile on my face.

"Thatta girl," Marla says. "That's what my customers like to see."

Marla directs me behind the counter, has me sign forms, then holds out a yellow apron. "Here, put this on. You can shadow me until your shift ends."

Yellow isn't really my color, but I hang the sunshiny thing around my neck and tie the wrap at my waist without complaint. Even though it's seven o'clock, there are still customers hanging out and ordering pastries. They're even drinking coffee this late, especially the ones who pull all-nighters.

The most all-nighters I see are lawyers. The ones who have to head to court in the morning or prepare for what they call depositions. Do you think the money they make is worth it for the amount of sleep they're missing? There's no way I could ever be a lawyer. I like my sleep too much.

After fifteen minutes, Marla hands me a white rag with antibacterial stuff on it and tells me to wipe off the tables.

I was really hoping to hide behind the counter all night until my shift was up, but Marla's having none of that. I'm just thankful she hasn't asked me to clean out the bathrooms so I shuffle over to the tables and start wiping them off.

I start cleaning the private nook where a couch and two cushy chairs are located, then I freeze. Sitting in the chair, reading, is none other than Nathan *Keener's-not-my-last-name* Greyson. He looks up and I can tell he's about as thrilled to see me as I am to see him. The cup stops short of his lips.

Ignoring the urge to confront him about spreading rumors about me, I hurriedly wipe his table before he sets whatever he's drinking back down.

"You missed a spot," Nathan mumbles. I huff. I did not miss a spot.

"All the tables are clean," I tell Marla back at the register.

She seems pleased as she does an eye scan of the café. For the next thirty minutes, Marla gives me the rundown on how to make the espressos, cold drinks, blended drinks, and tells me the particulars of some of her customers. She also explains how to use the cash register. I'm dizzy from the information overload, but I think I got it. Or at the very least I'll make it look like I got it.

"You think you can hold down the fort for five minutes while I call in an order for more cups?" Marla asks. "And don't forget to smile. Remember, the café is called Perk Me Up!"

Just call me the Smiling Barista Extraordinare. Well, not really—I don't know how to "garnish," as Marla puts it, with cinnamon, nutmeg, and other fancy stuff. I've been hanging out at Perk Me Up! ever since I moved in with my dad, so I pretty much know the basic routine. It's the non-basic that throws me off.

While I'm counting how many cups we have left, the door to the café opens.

My first real customer. I smile and look up then relax as I realize who my customer is.

My dad.

"Welcome to Perk Me Up!" I tell him in an overly formal tone. "Can I help you?"

He walks up to the counter and surveys the scene. "You look good as a working woman," he says, looking proud.

"Cut the crap. What do you want?"

I hear a gasp beside me. Oops, it's Marla. And she can't see I'm talking to my dad instead of a real customer. "Amy!" she chastises.

But when she reaches me, she breathes a sigh of relief.

"Boy, you've got tough employees," my dad says, then gives Marla a wink. "Okay, Amy, give me a large cup of your house coffee, black, with a shot of espresso."

"You're never gonna fall asleep," I tell him.

"Good. I've got a lot of work to do tonight."

It's a wonder my father isn't a lawyer. He never tells me the specifics of his work. I guess it's cool that he's got a top-secret job, so I don't bug him about working late.

I pour the mixture into a cup while Marla watches me closely. She smiles as I finish; then I hand it to my dad. He takes a sip right away, not even waiting for it to cool off. "*Best*-tasting coffee I've ever had in my life," he tells Marla, his overzealous reaction totally obvious.

I roll my eyes. "*Aba*, go sit down already."

"Why don't you join him," Marla says. "Your shift is over."

"I've only been here an hour. How can it be over?"

"That's our deal," my dad chimes in. "An hour a day on the weekdays, three hours on Sundays. I didn't want it to interfere with your schoolwork."

Eight hours a week isn't so bad, especially because I'll still have my Saturday nights free.

I hand Marla my yellow apron, but she says to bring it back tomorrow when I work. Then I grab my purse from the locked cabinet and sit down with my dad at one of the tables.

My dad takes out mail from his briefcase and starts rummaging through it. I'm craning my neck to see if there's a letter from Avi. It's been over two weeks since I've gotten one. It's unlike him.

"Well?" I ask.

My dad has this mischievous smile that gives it away.

I hold my hand out. "Give."

He holds out a letter and I snatch it out of his hand. My heart skips a beat and my stomach feels like little butterflies are flying around inside me as I run my fingers over the return address.

Since Avi and I have this long-distance relationship, I get insecure. When I'm in bed at night, thinking about how much I miss him, I wonder: Did he forget about me? Has he met someone else who's cuter or nicer or just…doesn't have as many hang-ups as me?

I'm feeling a bit better as I rip open the letter, but then notice my dad staring at me…gauging my reaction.

"Why don't you read it out loud," he suggests.

"Yeah, right," I say sarcastically. I stick the letter in my pocket, I'll read it later when I'm in bed…alone.

"Wait!" Marla calls out as we're about to leave. She's

holding a backpack. "Do you know that boy who was sitting on one of the chairs over there? He left this."

"It's Nathan's," I say. "I'm sure he'll realize it and come back to get it."

"Don't be silly, Amy," my dad says. "You can return it to him on the way home."

8

Deborah was a great prophetess of Israel, even led Israel
for a time (Judges 4:4). She ordered a man named Barak
(relation to me, perhaps?) to take ten thousand men into
battle. Barak told Deborah that he'd only do it if Debo-
rah came with him. Kind of parallels my life, doesn't it?
Also reinforces that men need women to back them up.

I want to protest, but the backpack is being shoved into
my hands. "Dad, I'm sure he'll come back to get it once he
realizes—"

"Amy, don't be a snob."

My mouth opens wide in shock. My own flesh and
blood just called me a snob. I head out the door and into
our condo building entrance. I wave to the doorman, who
buzzes me into the elevator banks.

"Amy, come back here," my dad says.

I put my hands on my hips. "I can't believe you, of all
people, called me a snob."

My dad never backs down. I guess being an ex-commando
makes you act like a tough guy in your personal as well as army

life. Occupational hazard. "Just because he doesn't look like the kids you hang out with doesn't mean you can't be friends with him."

"Dad, he told Kyle Sanderson I joined a dating service because I couldn't get a date for the Valentine's Dance."

Who's the snob now?

My dad looks concerned; his eyebrows are furrowed as he contemplates this new piece of information. Taking a deep breath, he tells me, "Then confront him about it."

Spoken like a true Israeli.

We're in the elevator, which has just reached our floor. Stepping off, I turn around to face my father and hold out Nathan's backpack (which weighs a ton, I might add). "You give it to him. Then you can ream him out for spreading rumors about your daughter."

"We'll go together."

Ooh, partners in crime. "Fine."

"Fine."

I follow him to Nathan's aunt and uncle's condo right down the hall from us. My dad knocks obnoxiously loud, like he doesn't know the power of his own strength. *That's my dad.*

Mr. Keener opens the door, but doesn't invite us in.

"Nathan left his backpack in the café," my dad says. "Amy wanted to bring it back to him."

Mr. Keener smiles and opens the door. "You can go give it to him. He's in the guest room. It's the second door on the right."

My dad puts his hand on the small of my back and

pushes me forward. I've never been into their condo. Mr. and Mrs. Keener keep pretty much to themselves. I step inside the foyer. I'm feeling awkward so I'm glad my dad is backing me up.

A cell phone rings; it's my dad's ring tone. The national anthem of Israel. Dorky, but totally *him*. He's still in the hallway as he answers the call. "Sorry, *motek*, I have to take this," he says as he waves and leaves me in the Keeners' condo.

Oh, just great.

So now I'm faced with going into Nathan's room. All alone. With absolutely no backup.

Mr. Keener waves me toward Nathan's room. Okay, I'll do it. I'm not afraid of that guy. In fact, after I shove his backpack at him, I'm going to give him a piece of my mind.

Because nobody makes a fool out of Amy Nelson-Barak.

I walk with purpose to the second door on the right. The door is closed, so I have to knock. Looking back, I see Mr. Keener hasn't followed. I knock lightly at first with the hand not holding the backpack. No response. I knock a little harder.

After I get no response again, I think he might not be home after all. Which is a good thing, I think. I mean, I want to confront him and everything but I'm not sure I want to do it on his turf. I know the advantage to warfare. On your own turf you have the upper hand.

I check the doorknob to see if it's locked. Nope. I turn the knob and crack the door open so I can peek inside.

Nathan's in the room, but he's listening to his iPod while banging a pencil against a binder, so he can't hear me.

Sure enough, as soon as I look at his face I catch two green eyes narrowing at me.

"I can see you," he says.

Damn. I open the door wide and walk in, watching as he takes the earphones out of his ears. "You left your backpack at Perk Me Up! I brought it as a goodwill gesture."

The guy just shrugs. *Thanks* would have been nice. Nathan is in dire need of etiquette lessons.

As I drop his backpack, I scan the room. It's obviously the guest room. Old bookshelves line the side wall and a pullout bed is open and takes up most of the room. Nathan is leaning on the bed, against the back, just staring at me.

"Who's the girl?" I ask, picking up a picture of a cute blonde girl in a bikini with short hair and abs I can't even imagine having. "Your sister?"

Nathan pushes his glasses up his nose and says, "It's my girlfriend."

Yeah, right. There is absolutely no way this is Nathan's girlfriend. I'd bet my dog on it.

"What's her name?" I ask, curiosity getting the best of me.

"Bicky."

Wait. What did he say? "Becky?" I ask. The other alternative is downright ludicrous.

"Bicky," he says again.

"*Bicky?*"

"Now you're acting Barbie all over again."

"Was she born with that name or is it a nickname?" I ask, ignoring the insult.

Nathan slides off the bed and snatches the picture out of my hand. "Her name is Bicky. No nickname. Just Bicky."

While he shoves the picture into his half-zipped suitcase, I say, "You accuse me of being so Barbie when you're the one who's deliberately spreading untrue rumors about me just so you could seem cool."

"I did no such thing," he says. "And I definitely don't want to hang around with your friends, if that's what you mean."

"You told Kyle I joined a dating service. For your information...and not that it's any of your business, but I signed my dad up."

Nathan shrugs, as if falsely tarnishing my reputation is no biggie.

"Why do you hate me so much?"

He rubs his hand on top of his shaggy, light brown hair that resembles the color of maple syrup, and sighs. "I don't hate you, Amy. I just hate people like you."

"Same difference," I say, then storm out of the condo. When I stomp into my own place, my dad is sitting at the dining room table, still on the phone as he shuffles through some papers.

Men. I feel the taste for revenge. I head to the back office, where the computer is, and type in *www.pjsn.com*. It prompts me to type in my login name and password.

I have fifty-five new people who left messages on my

dad's profile and the two women I asked out for my dad responded. Wow. The human resources worker, Kelly, would love to do coffee, how about next week? and the lawyer, Wendy, says she's looking for an American guy so she's not interested.

Good. I didn't want a lawyer to be my stepmom anyway. Lawyers probably follow all the rules and regs in life. That's not my style. I live inside the gray areas and love it.

I e-mail the human resources lady back and ask her to meet me (aka my dad) at Perk Me Up! tomorrow night at seven.

As I settle into the chair, I hear a crinkling sound from my back pocket. Oh my God. I can't believe I forgot with all the Nathan-and-my-dad commotion to open Avi's letter. Is my forgetfulness a betrayal of our relationship?

Uncrinkling it, I sink back in my bed and open the envelope.

"Sorry, Avi." He can't hear me, but maybe my conscience can.

As I unfold the letter, my heartbeat starts racing.

Amy,

You know I'm not good with letters, but I promised to write so I'm writing. I'm assigned to a new army base, but I can't tell you where it is. Top secret stuff. I can tell you that I shot a new gun today. I know you hate guns, but this one was cool. It shoots around corners. We run every day until I think my legs are going to fall off. Tomorrow my unit will be dropped off in the Negev in the middle of the night to see if we can navigate with nothing but the stars to guide us through the desert. I guess that's it. If I survive desert training I'll write you again. You know I miss you, don't you?

Avi

I hold the letter to my chest, concentrating on the last sentence. *You know I miss you, don't you?* Avi isn't one of those sappy guys; he's guarded because he lost his brother in a bombing and hasn't let himself open up, be vulnerable, and grieve. And I know he doesn't want me to wait around for him while he spends his required three years in the Israeli military, so he doesn't write romantic and mushy letters.

I don't want a romantic and mushy guy, anyway. I want Avi. Oh, I know I'm not going to even see him until the summer when I go back to Israel. I'm not holding my breath that he'll be waiting for me. Okay, I am. But I'm not admitting it publicly.

Leaning over my nightstand, I open the drawer and pull out Avi's silver chain link bracelet. He gave it to me after we started dating this past summer. I also pull out a picture of him. It was after our last official date, when he gave me Mutt and a sushi dinner. I snatched a photo with my dad's camera right before our last goodbye.

I stare at the picture, him with his mocha eyes and thick head of dark hair to match. Not to mention his signature half-smile, which can make my heart stop. There is no way the girls in Israel are going to leave him alone; that's a given. It scares me and brings out my worst insecurities. I'm not pretty enough, my boobs are too big, I'm not skinny enough.

Ugh, I hate when I pick myself apart and focus on the negatives. Avi likes me for who I am. I know he does.

Kissing his picture would be the dorkiest thing. I'd never do that. But I do clutch his picture to my chest and hug it. It's still dorky, but less so than actually kissing it.

"Amy, I'm sorry but it was an important call."

Great, now my dad is invading my personal space and witnessed me hugging a picture. The only thing keeping me from telling him how important knocking on a teenager's door is the revenge date I'm setting him up on. "You know what your problem is?" I tell him.

"What."

"You think work is more important than your personal life."

He takes life way too seriously, but I'm trying to help him loosen up and not be such a stiff. It's the work part that worries me. I swear he's gonna have a heart attack one of these days if he doesn't let up on the work hours.

He walks closer to my bed and I slip the picture of Avi and his letter under my pillow.

"I have responsibilities, Amy. Ones I've committed to long ago."

"Yeah, yeah," I say, sitting up. "I've heard the spiel before. What now, the president of the United States needs you to act as his bodyguard?"

"The Secret Service does that."

"Then what's so important?" I ask him.

"I have to go out of town. That's what the call was about. It can't be postponed, not this time."

Cool. So I'll get the condo all to myself? The possibilities are endless.

"When?" I say a little too eagerly.

"On Friday morning. I'll be back on Sunday."

Two whole nights without parental figures! Brighter times are definitely ahead. "Can I use your car?"

"Only to go to your mother's house. That's where you'll be staying. I just got off the phone with her. You can have my car to drive to her place."

Nope, not okay. "I am *not* staying with Mom and Marc. What would I do with Mutt? Besides, I think Marc is allergic to both of us."

"We'll put him in a kennel."

I wish he were talking about Marc, but I'm not that lucky. This time I stand up, ready for battle. "First of all, Mutt and I are a package deal. He is not going to a kennel. Period, end of story."

It takes me exactly fifty-six minutes to convince my dad I'm old enough to stay at the condo without parents.

Brighter times are definitely ahead.

9

*Kosher question #2: You can't mix milk and meat because
God commanded "You shall not boil a kid (baby lamb)
in its mother's milk" (Exodus 23:19). So why can't I mix
milk with chicken? You can't milk a chicken.*

"Why do you keep glancing at the door every two seconds?" Marla asks me the next day at work.

Umm…maybe it's because my dad's date is gonna be here any second, followed by my dad who still doesn't know he's going on a date. He thinks Marla needs to talk to him about my work schedule. I made up some ridiculous story to get him into the café at seven o'clock.

"I'm watching for my dad," I tell my boss guiltily.

The door to the café opens. It's a woman I've never seen before. Is it Kelly, my dad's date? Or is it someone else? Kelly wrote in her e-mail that she has strawberry blonde hair. This woman kind of has strawberry blonde hair, although it's really frizzy and she needs some expensive hair products to help tame that mane of hers. That picture she posted online was with her hair straight, but maybe she forgot to flatiron it today.

She walks up to the counter and suddenly I'm feeling self-conscious, like I have to impress the woman. "Are you Kelly?" I ask.

The woman shakes her Brillo pad head. "No."

"Oh, good."

When she frowns at me, I try and recover quick. "Can I take your order?"

She looks up at our board of specialty coffees, taking her time. I have the urge to give her a snoring sound (I'm good at those) but don't think Marla will appreciate my humor. So I wait with a smile on my face. And wait.

And wait.

And wait.

I swear, any more of this waiting and I'm going to frown. My mouth can't take all this fake smiling. I start humming, but I don't even realize it until the woman looks down at me with a stern expression. Seriously, thank goodness this woman isn't my dad's strawberry blonde date.

The door dings. Another customer. "Are you ready?" I ask the woman who can't make up her mind. I could just see her as my stepmom, me waiting for her to pick me up from school, taking forever to pick out groceries, and waiting for her to order a simple spicy tuna roll from Hanabi.

Looking around her, another woman who could pass for strawberry blonde walks up to the counter. I suck in my breath. This woman is really large. And I'm being nice.

Maybe the picture she posted was pre-weight gain. My dad is a workout and health nut, and this woman looks like she's snacked on a few too many Kit Kats if you know what I mean. She has a friendly face, though. Hey, maybe Dad can put her on a boot camp diet plan and she'd lose those extra pounds in no time at all.

Ignoring the wishy-washy lady, I ask the overweight one, "Are you Kelly?"

"No. But I'd like a large caramel latte with whipped cream."

I keep up the Perk Me Up! smile, although I'm tempted to suggest the skim latte instead of the caramel one. While I'm ringing her up, the wishy-washy lady signals to me she's ready. Can't she see I'm ringing up someone else?

Marla is in the office and I don't want her to think I can't take care of the customers. I turn to the wishy-washer. "Did you decide?"

"What's the calorie count of the medium vanilla coffee? Is it the same as the regular?"

Is she kidding me? I look under the counter to see if there's a calorie listing for the drinks, but there isn't. Now I don't know what to do. Should I make the other lady's drink or call Marla to help?

I look at my watch. It's seven on the dot. Kelly will be here any second. My dad will be here any second.

And Miss Wishy-Washy is worried about a calorie count.

I knock on the door to the office and call Marla out to the register. I hurry to make the large caramel latte while

Marla takes care of the frizzy-haired, high-maintenance customer. The chime rings on the door and a woman walks into the café who definitely looks like Kelly's PJSN profile pic.

She scans the café, then sits down at a vacant table to wait for my unsuspecting dad.

Sure enough, my dad walks in the door next. My heart is palpitating a hundred beats a second right now. My dad waves to me and walks up to the register. Kelly must recognize him from the picture I posted on his profile. She moves up behind him and is about to tap him on the shoulder.

"I have to tell you something," I say at the same time Kelly taps him and says, "Ron?"

He turns to her. "Can I help you?"

"Dad, it's important."

He puts his fingertips together on one hand and moves it up and down, the unique Israeli sign for *wait a second*. The problem is, I can't wait a second. I need to tell him that, even though he's unaware of it, he's on his first PJSN date.

"I'm Kelly. Are you Ron?" Kelly asks.

"Yes."

"From the Professional Jewish Singles Network?"

Pause.

"Um…could you hold that thought for one second," my dad says to Kelly. Then he turns to me. "Tell me what this is all about, Amy. Right. Now. I'm assuming Marla doesn't want to talk to me about adjusting your work schedule."

"*Aba*, you're going to laugh when I tell you this."

"I doubt it."

Kelly looks upset and embarrassed. "Am I missing something here?"

Okay, it's time to fess up. I thought it'd be easier than it is. I have the urge to hide in a dark corner. "I set up the date. I'm his daughter," I tell her.

Getting it, Kelly steps back. "Oh." She adjusts the Coach bag hanging on her shoulder. "Well, that makes me look stupid."

"Actually, it makes me look stupid," I tell her.

"And me," my dad chimes in. "I'll tell you what, Kelly. Why don't we sit down and have my daughter serve us the most expensive drinks in the place. It'll be her treat."

Kelly shrugs and nods her head in agreement. "Sounds good to me."

It doesn't sound good to me at all!

"I'm hungry, actually. How about one of the scones?" my dad asks. I'm adding the bill in my head, knowing I'll have to work at least two more hours in order to pay for the food bill.

"Scones sound wonderful," Kelly says, smiling. "Don't they have Eli's cheesecake, too? Grab me a slice of that, would you, dear?"

I'm not liking Kelly with the strawberry blonde hair as much as my dad seems to like her. Teaching me a lesson is not how I imagined this date going. My dad sits down with Kelly while I bring them over Double Dutch Coffee Delight drinks. (I add a couple extra shots of espresso as a bonus…I hope they both are up all night and can't sleep.) Those specialty drinks are four dollars and twenty-five cents each, along with the two-dollar-and-fifty-five-cent cheesecake and two-dollar-and-thirty-five-cent scones.

As if my day isn't disastrous enough, when Marla tells me to sweep the floor of the café I find Nathan at his usual spot in the corner. "You got caught in one of your lies, Barbie?" Nathan says. "I have a piece of advice. Next time you set your dad up on a date, you should probably tell him about it beforehand."

I shoot him a nasty glare. "At least I have parents," I say, then want to take back my words right after they've left my mouth. Nathan's face goes ashen and he starts packing up his stuff.

Maybe his parents are dead or in the hospital somewhere. I'm a jerk. "I'm sorry," I quickly say.

As he shoves the last book into his backpack, he looks up at me. "No you're not." Then he leaves me standing here while he storms out of the café, leaving me to pick up his used cup which is still three-quarters of the way full with tea. Now I'm feeling even worse than before.

I glance over at my dad, who's shaking hands with Kelly. She exits the café, leaving my dad alone at the table until I saunter up to him and say, "So?"

He looks up at me from his chair. "So what?"

"How was the date?"

"Fine."

Fine is probably the most non-committal and non-descriptive word in the English language. I hate the word *fine*. It doesn't even mean anything. I try a different approach, one that can't be answered with a "fine." "Are you gonna see her again?"

"Maybe."

Great, another non-descriptive word. "Did you get her number?"

My dad stands now, which is not a good thing because he's way taller than me. "Listen to me, Amy, and listen good. Don't set me up on another date without my knowledge or you'll find yourself without a cell phone. Got it?"

"Fine."

10

Rosh Hashanah: Two nights of huge festive meals.
Hanukkah: Eat foods cooked in oil.
Passover: The Haggadah (Passover prayer book) specifically
says, Eat The Festive Meal.
Sukkot: Build a sukkah and invite friends to eat in it.
Yom Kippur: Eat three meals at once
to make up for the day just fasted.
I see a pattern here.
Why are so many Jewish holidays centered around food?

Since my dad went out of town this morning, Jessica invited me over for Shabbat dinner. So after school I go home, walk Mutt, then take a cab to Jessica's. I might also add that Nathan ignored me the entire day. Even when I tried to apologize again, he turned around and blatantly dissed me.

"Come in, Amy," Jessica's mom says when she opens the door to their six-flat. "Jessica is in her room."

I climb the familiar whitewashed staircase and catch Jessica sitting at her desk, punching the keyboard of her computer. "You're not checking Mitch's e-mail again, are you?"

Without looking at me she responds, "You bet I am.

He has no clue. I check them all and mark them as 'unread' e-mail."

"Jess, break up with him if you don't trust him."

Jess swivels her chair around to face me. "He told me he loved me on New Year's Eve, Amy. I haven't had a guy tell me he loved me since That Guy."

That Guy is Michael Greenberg, who Jessica lost her virginity to last year. He blew her off right after their big night together and she's been insecure about guys ever since. She won't even give me, her bestest friend in the entire world, details about what happened with Michael. I can't even say his name without her walking out of the room.

"Did he tell you he loved you in the heat of passion?"

"His hands were under my shirt."

Okay, so I'm not going to state the obvious. He gave her the ol' "I love you, let's get it on" crap. I look back at her and know she doesn't want to talk about it anymore.

I look inside Jessica's closet to see what new clothes she's gotten that I can borrow. I pick out a vintage gray shirt with pink writing. "Where did you get this?"

"I have no clue. My mom got it for me."

"It's cool." As always, I make myself at home. Best friends share clothes, secrets, and beauty tips. I guess we also share guys because I dated Mitch for about a millisecond before he started dating Jessica. Taking my own shirt off, I try on her gray one. It fits, except when I look in her long mirror on the back of her door my nipples stick out because the fabric of the shirt is too thin.

Depressed, I pull the shirt off and study my bra-covered boobs in the mirror.

"What are you doing?" Jess asks.

I hold my arms at my sides and look down at my pink lacy bra. "Do my boobs sag in this bra?" Testing what it would look like if they were perkier, I cup the bottom of my boobs and lift them up.

"Now they're too close to your chin." Jess lets out a frustrated sigh. "I wish I had your boobs. Guys *love* your boobs."

"They droop," I say, my hands letting go of them.

"How can they not, they weigh what…five pounds each?"

I'll have you know I've never weighed my boobs. And I'm sure they don't weigh more than two pounds each. I turn to my best friend. "Jess, you have perfect, perky boobs."

"Otherwise known as virtually non-existent," Jess says. "They only look perfect because I bought this Fantasy Bra last week." She pulls up her shirt to show me a padded pushup bra that's more padded than my mom's down winter coat. "I need this in order to look like I have *something*."

The door to Jessica's room flies open. It's her twelve-year-old annoying and testosterone-charged brother Ben. His eyes go wide at the sight of us in our bras. I screech and hold my hands out to cover my chest.

"Get out, you little creep!" Jess yells, pulling her shirt back down.

"Are you guys comparing boobies?" Ben says while laughing. "Amy, are those real?"

Jessica and I both grab pillows off her bed and fling them at the door while Ben slams it shut. "By the way, dinner's ready," he says, still laughing.

When we enter the dining room a few minutes later, Jess flicks her brother hard on the back of the head before sitting down.

"Ow!"

"If you don't knock next time, I'm going to take a picture of you while you're in the shower and e-mail it to your entire school."

"That's enough," Mr. Katz says, putting on his *kippah* and motioning for Ben to put his on, too.

In the kitchen, Jess and I help place soup bowls filled with matzoh ball soup on the table.

Mrs. Katz sets up two Shabbat candlesticks with candles in them and takes matches out of a decanter on the credenza. "Amy, would you like to do the honors?"

Me? I usually watch while Jessica or her mom lights the candles and does the Hebrew prayer. "Are you sure?"

"Absolutely."

The entire room is silent as I clear my throat. Striking the match, I light both candles. When they're lit, I cover my eyes with my palms and say, "*Baruch ata Adonai Eloheinu, melech ha'olam, asher kid'shanu b'mitzvotav v'tzivanu l'hadlik ner shel Shabbat.* Blessed are You, Lord our God, King of the universe, who has made us holy through His commandments and commanded us to kindle the Sabbath light."

I take my seat at the table, abandoning the candles in the corner, when Mrs. Katz says, "Amy, did you make a wish?"

"A wish?"

"Yes, over the candles. It's our custom to do the prayer, then make a silent wish to God. Or a thank-you to God...whatever your heart feels like saying."

Standing up and walking back to the bright yellow burning candles, I cover my eyes again and think about what I want to say.

"Ask God for Ben to accidentally have his orthodontist wire his mouth shut," Jess says.

"Ask for Jess to grow boobs," Ben's voice chimes in.

Ignoring both of them, I say to God, *Please take care of my Safta in Israel. She has cancer and needs your help. And also, thanks for giving me this family to have dinner with tonight so I'm not alone.*

I look up, expecting everyone to be staring at me and to ask me what I wished for. But they're not; they respect my private Shabbat wish and thanks to God. I love Jessica and her family. Even Ben.

"I saw Amy's boobies upstairs," Ben says, then wags his eyebrows up and down at me.

Okay, maybe not Ben.

Mrs. Katz slams her hand on the table. "Can I please have a respectful Shabbat?"

"Listen to your mother," Mr. Katz says. He stands while picking up the silver Shabbat wine cup and pours the red wine until it's almost overflowing. "*Baruch ata Adonai Eloheinu, melech ha'olam, boray pri ha-gafen.* Amen."

After he takes a sip from the cup, he passes it around for everyone else to take a sip. Ben puts on a big show of gulping down the wine, but then he coughs so it splatters across the white tablecloth.

Jess rolls her eyes, takes a sip, and passes the cup to me. I'm not a wine drinker, but this wine is so sweet it's like drinking sugary children's cough syrup.

Ben lifts the embroidered cloth cover off of the challah, the Shabbat bread which is expertly braided at the kosher bakery down the street. "*Baruch ata Adonai Eloheinu, melech ha'olam, ha-motze lechem min ha'aretz,*" he says, then makes a big show of singing, "Aaa, aaah, maaaaaaiiiiinnn."

Jess and I mumble, "Amen."

Ben tears a chunk of the challah off and tosses everyone a small piece from the chunk. I think he tried tossing it into my cleavage, but I'm not sure. And when it comes to tossing a piece to Jess, he whips it at her. I think the kid needs to go to therapy, or at least be locked up until he turns eighteen.

"How is the conversion class going, Amy?" Mr. Katz asks me as he takes a spoonful of matzoh ball soup.

"Good. Rabbi Glassman is really nice."

Mrs. Katz puts her hand over her husband's. "He married us, you know. Twenty-two years ago."

I wonder if Rabbi Glassman will officiate my wedding one day. Even though he's not Orthodox, he won't officiate a marriage between a Jewish person and a non-Jew.

He's kind of strict about that, even refused to marry his own sister because she married a Christian guy. I want to marry someone Jewish because I think it will head off lots of arguments. It's important that my kids are Jewish; it's important that my family doesn't eat pork or shellfish...or mix meat and milk products.

"Are you going to the youth group meeting tomorrow?" Mrs. Katz asks.

Jessica nods her head and says, "Are you coming, Amy?"

"I wasn't planning on it."

"You should go. It's fun."

After dinner, Jess and I convince her parents to let us go back to my place to crash. We spend the rest of the evening Ben-less, talking about boys and bras and books until we're tired. Then we take out ice cream from the freezer and watch movies on TV until I convince Jessica to call Mitch.

He isn't answering his cell, so she tries his house. Unfortunately, she gets reamed out by Mitch's dad for calling past eleven o'clock. He doesn't even tell her if Mitch is home or not.

What do two parentless teenagers do at eleven at night? I have a brilliant idea. "Let's call my cousin in Israel. It's eight hours ahead there."

Before Jess can tell me it's a horrible idea, I start dialing the gazillion digits to get access to the Israeli phone system. "Allo?" my Doda Yucky answers.

"Doda Yucky, it's Amy," I yell into the receiver.

"Ah, Amy'leh. *Mah nishmah*?" The woman thinks I'm

fluent in Hebrew, but really my dad told me *mah nishmah* means "how is everything?" It's a staple phrase for Israelis.

"Great. Is Osnat there?"

"She's right here. Give your *aba* my love, *tov?*"

"*Tov.*"

"Amy?" Osnat asks.

"Yeah, it's your American cousin. Remember me?"

"How could I forget. Our sheep still has a Mohawk from when you shaved it."

Ha, ha. Very funny. Okay, so my sheep-shearing skills are definitely lacking, but I did make a valiant effort. "*Mah nishmah?*" I ask her.

"*Ah, evreet shelach mitzuyan.*"

"Okay, cut the Hebrew. You know I have no clue what you're saying. How's Avi?"

"Looking hot."

"You've seen him?"

"Yeah. Why, hasn't he called you since his basic training was over?"

No. "I'm sure he was busy." He wrote that he'd be in basic training for another week. I wonder what he's doing back home. Even more, I wonder why he hasn't called. You know what they say: if they're not into you, they don't call. If they're into you, they'll find the time.

My stomach muscles clench up, but I continue talking to Osnat and then talk to *Safta,* my grandmother, who tells me the doctors think her tumor shrunk since her last set of chemo treatments. She insists she's doing fine, but her voice is weaker than I remember. I promise to call next week and she promises she'll stay healthy and strong until I come to Israel for summer break.

Jess is thumbing through my CD collection, looking more depressed than I am. I come up with an idea. "Try texting Mitch."

"I tried before. He ignored it."

I grab her phone and start texting.

Jess sits on the bed next to me. "What are you doing?"

"Getting your boyfriend's attention," I tell her. Mitch is obsessed with his cell phone. He'll for sure have it with him. If he's ignoring Jess on purpose, I'll kill him.

Me: Mitch, it's Amy. Jess is XOXOing another dude
Mitch: What?
Me: Just kidding. Where R U?
Mitch: At a movie w/friends. Can't talk.
Me: Call your gf tomorrow. Or else.
Mitch: U don't scare me, Amy.
Me: Y not?
Mitch: Bark worse than bite.
Me: I don't bite.
Mitch: I dated U. U bite.

I turn off the phone and look up at Jess. "He said he'll call you tomorrow."

"Really?" she asks, looking hopeful. "Where is he?"

"At a movie with friends."

"I talked to him earlier. He didn't say anything about a movie. Since when can't I go with him and his friends to a movie?"

I shrug. I can't figure out my own boyfriend. How am I supposed to figure out hers?

I lie in bed later thinking about all the promises I forgot to get from Avi. Maybe I'm delirious thinking he's waiting for me to come back to Israel. If he's not thinking of me, why am I so obsessed with him?

11

> *"When a woman at childbirth bears a male,*
> *she shall be unclean seven days...*
> *If she bears a female, she shall be unclean two weeks."*
> *(Leviticus 12:2-5)*
> *Umm...does this mean boys are viewed*
> *as cleaner than females? Has God seen the boys' restroom*
> *at Chicago Academy lately?*

"Do you know if it's a boy or girl?"

It's Sunday and I'm in the 'burbs with my mom. We're sitting in her car, heading to a maternity-clothes shop. She looked so excited about this little excursion; I couldn't say no.

My mom rubs the bump in her stomach, like a prego person in the movies would. "We want it to be a surprise."

"What if it's twins?" I ask her.

When she smiles at me, the corners of her light blue eyes crinkle. Isn't she too old to have a baby? "There was only one heartbeat. No twins."

The baby is due in six months and already my mom's stomach looks like a small bowling ball. I can't believe I haven't noticed it before. Maybe she's been trying to hide it with those ponchos she's overly fond of lately.

When we drive up to a place called Modern Maternity I feel stupid. I'm seventeen years old. I could seriously be a mother myself.

"Marc and I both want you to be involved in this pregnancy," she says. "It's important to us."

My mom's not Jewish, but she definitely has the Jewish guilt thing down pat.

I put on a huge, toothy smile. I'm probably overdoing it, but the reality is I want my mom to be happy. "I'm so happy for you," I gush. "And I want to be a part of this new family, too!"

"Amy, I'm your mom. I can see right through you."

We're still sitting in the car. I watch her face turn from elation to unhappiness in a matter of seconds. Oh, no. I gotta talk to her before she starts crying. "Mom, I *am* happy for you and Marc. It's just weird for me. First the wedding, now the baby. I just need time to get used to it, okay?"

I remember back to when my mom took me to my first ballet lesson. I'd begged for her to sign me up and practically dragged her to Miss Gertie's Dance Studio where Jessica was already taking lessons. My mom paid the hefty tuition, bought me ballet slippers and a cute leotard, and off we went to the first class. Only there was one problem: I refused to go inside the studio. For some unknown reason (even to me) I cried in the car until my mom dragged me kicking and screaming into that studio.

She forced me to go.

In retaliation, I sat in the corner of the studio and refused to move even one pink ballet-slippered foot the entire time. This routine continued lesson after lesson until the costumes came in for the recital. My class danced to a song called "The Buzy Bees." We were little bees with black and yellow sparkly sequined leotards and black springy sparkly antennas. What can I say, all those sparkles would turn any reluctant kid into an instant ballerina just waiting to go on stage. The day those costumes came in, I stood up from my usual spot and danced and buzzed around as if I was making up for lost time.

Those ballet lessons made me learn one thing:

My mom is a patient parent beyond belief. And she'll wait anything out until I cave.

"Amy, I know it's not easy for you. Too many changes in such a short time." She looks up at the sign to Modern Maternity. "Should we just go back home? Or go bra shopping for you? I can do this another day."

"No, we're already here. You might as well get some clothes that won't strangle the baby." Besides, I don't want to go bra shopping with my mom. She'll probably pick out those big hefty white ones that resemble tablecloths with straps.

Mom needs no further encouragement. She's out of the car as if someone was pushing her enlarged butt forward. I swear, my mom used to have a body an aerobics instructor would be jealous of. Now…well, let's just say she's changed a *lot*.

I follow her into the store, silently hoping the salesperson doesn't mistake me for the customer.

"Can I help you ladies?" the short and perky salesperson asks, looking from my mom to me and back.

My mom touches her stomach again. "Well, I'm about three months along now and am outgrowing my clothes already."

The lady claps her hands together. "Are we looking for casual or business attire...or do you need something for a specific occasion?"

I'd like to cut the word "we" from the woman's vocabulary.

"Casual. And business."

While the lady shows my mom around the store, I follow in silence. To be honest, though, some of the clothes aren't too bad. And before long my mom is trying the stuff on, making me go with her into the dressing room.

On the bench I catch sight of something weird. It's like a cream-colored pouch with strings coming out of it. "I think someone left something in here," I tell the saleslady, pointing to the strange object.

"No, there's one in every dressing room. It's to strap to your stomach to make you look five to six months pregnant."

I can't help the giggle that escapes my mouth. My mom shushes me, then closes the dressing room door.

"Can I try it on?" I ask.

Before my mom can stop me, I pick up my shirt, tie the pouch around my waist, and pull my shirt back down.

"That's not really the image I want of my seventeen-year-old daughter," Mom says, eyeing me rub my tummy like she does.

I wonder what it would be like to be pregnant. A baby growing inside your body until it can survive on its own. Turning sideways, I check myself out in the mirror. Do I want kids? I mean, I feel sorry for my parents that they have to deal with me. Sometimes I think I'm not normal, that I'm long overdue for a psychotherapist to straighten me out. Then at other times I feel like everyone else is a mashed-potato nutcase and I'm the only sane one.

Maybe Mom's banking on this new kid to be the normal one, the one who's freak-out resistant.

I stare at my mom's stomach as she tries on a black and white suit with a stretchy panel in the front of the pants. It makes me realize what a big deal this must be for her. She's not just getting big; she's creating another human being, one she'll be responsible for forever.

"You can touch my stomach if you want," she says.

I do, but I don't. I remember I used to lay my head on her stomach and laugh as I heard gurgling noises coming from it. Now there's a baby growing inside there...

I guess she senses my hesitation, because she takes my hand and places it on her bulging tummy. "Can you feel it moving?" I ask.

"Not yet."

I gaze at my hand on her belly, close to my half brother or sister. As much as I know it's weird for my mom to have a kid, I'm feeling unusually protective of it right now. I pull my hand away; this is getting a little too weird for me.

She tries on a big white shirt with an arrow pointing down saying *Future Physician*. "What do you think?" she asks, holding her arms out wide to give me the full view.

"I think it's weak sauce."

"Weak sauce?" she says, scrunching up her face in confusion. "New slang I don't know about?"

"You know...same as lame. It's all about the sauce. If it's bad sauce, nobody likes it."

"Is this one lame sauce?"

I don't correct her and tell her it's *weak* sauce, not *lame* sauce.

Now she's holding out one that says *Almost done*.

"You can get it, but I'm not going out with you in public if you're wearing it. Don't they have one saying *I'm a Dorky Mom*?"

"I didn't see that one on the racks," she says, teasing me.

In the end, she picks out a pants suit for work, one dress, two pairs of jeans, and three T-shirts that don't have writing on them. I swear, before my mom was married and actually had a job, she dressed like she was a Vogue model. She knew everything about fashion and taught me so much. Now, my mom got married, quit her job, and seriously does not know what's in. I hope after the baby is born she'll change back into the same mom I had before.

"Are you staying over for dinner?" she asks when we're on the way back to her house.

"Sorry, can't. I'm going to some Jewish teen group thing with Jessica."

"You sure about this Jewish route, Amy? Marc and I

were discussing it the other day, and we just don't understand this sudden interest in conversion."

Mom doesn't understand that during my trip to Israel last summer I changed. It's like I found a missing piece of myself. It's a small piece, but sometimes I feel like when I find the missing pieces of myself I get closer to being whole. "It's not sudden, Mom."

"What does your father say? From what I know, he's not all that religious himself."

I look out the window, fighting the urge to argue with her. Converting to Judaism is something I feel strongly about. It has nothing to do with my dad or my mom. It has everything to do with me. To argue and try to make her see my side is pointless. My mom has her own opinions about organized religion and I don't share her view.

When *Safta* gave me a Jewish star pendant, I felt something I'd never felt before. A connection to people I had previously not acknowledged. And when I climbed Masada, it really hit me. My dad is Jewish, so half of me is Jewish. To ignore it suddenly felt like it would be dissing a part of who I am. I admit, learning about Judaism and reading the Tanakh (that would be the Torah and learning about the numerous Prophets) isn't easy. And, to be honest, I don't totally agree with or understand the Torah.

Rabbi Glassman encourages discussion, even disagreements. Which is great, because I'm disagreeable by nature. I question everything, like why Abraham really was going to kill his son. And it's obvious men wrote the Bible (it's a bit male-centered if I do say so myself.) But did the stories actually happen or were they made up?

"Dad supports me."

"But can't they consider you Jewish because your father is? It's seems silly to have you go through months of classes—"

"They're not *making* me do it, Mom." She just doesn't get it. Or maybe she doesn't want to get it. "I don't *have* to convert. I *want* to convert. Just...leave it alone, okay?"

Mom shrugs. "Okay, okay. I just want you to be happy."

"Then stop nagging me about religion. Nag me about something else instead."

Looking at me sideways, my mom smiles. Oops, I should never have said that. Because...you guessed it, she takes me to Sally's Intimate Boutique on the other side of town to get me fitted for bras.

Mom drives me back to the condo in the city after the bra run. I kiss her goodbye, get out of the car, and attempt to hide the girly pink bag under my arm. It's gotten so cold I pull my coat tight around me, but catch sight of Nathan standing on the curb with a bouquet of yellow tulips in his hand.

I'm still watching Nathan as my mom drives off. When the public bus heading to Evanston stops at the corner, Nathan gets on without a backward glance.

Hmm.

I wonder if he's going to see Binky...I mean Bicky. Not that I believe he's actually dating that girl in the picture in his room.

I still haven't figured him out. Why is he staying at his aunt and uncle's house? If it's *not* temporary, why is he still

91

living out of his suitcase? If it's *not* temporary, why is he going to my school? The whole thing doesn't add up.

Shaking thoughts of Nathan from my head, I run up to my condo before my dad gets home. Hurriedly, I check my dad's still-open PJSN account. The only problem is he'll kill me if I set him up on another date. I have to come up with another scheme, something creative.

I've heard about speed dating, where a person goes on a bunch of three-minute dates in one night. Hmm…maybe I can convince Marla to host one of them at Perk Me Up! one night. I must admit I have the best ideas.

My dad walks in the door just as I'm closing out the PJSN account. He asks me about my weekend without him. I ask him about his trip. We eat dinner together while playing *shesh besh*, which is Hebrew for backgammon. It's something we both like to play. We even have a little rivalry going on.

I answer the phone when it rings after dinner, knowing before I even check the caller ID that it's Jessica. "I need best friend advice," Jess says.

"Me, too. I need to know what I should wear tonight." I mean, I haven't been to a youth group meeting in…well, never.

"I thought you were going to wear your Fuego jeans and that heather-gray top you got last week at Saks."

I lay down on my bed in frustration, petting Mutt who just jumped on my stomach and almost knocked the wind out of me. "I was, but decided against it. I was thinking about wearing my long print skirt and a plain white shirt."

There's a big huff on the other end of the line. "Amy, you don't have to dress religious for the group."

"Come over and help me pick something to wear tonight. Please? I'll do your makeup for you and listen to your Mitch problems at the same time."

Jessica loves when I do her makeup. She will absolutely come over. I know her weakness is the two Ms—Mitch and makeup. For the double Ms, she'll go through the torture of finding a parking spot on the overcrowded Chicago streets.

"Um…I'm picking up Miranda Cohen first," Jess says.

"Miranda Cohen?" I ask. "The girl who hyperventilated when we ran the mile in gym last year?" Poor Miranda. The Diet Coke she drinks just doesn't erase the other crap from her system.

"Miranda's in the youth group."

So? I'm not best friends with Miranda, but I'd rather hang with her than Roxanne. "Jess, I need your help. Bring Miranda."

"I don't want to talk about Mitch in front of her, Amy."

"Okay, so here's my advice on the boyfriend front. Give Mitch some space and let him come after you. Ignore him for a bit. He thrives on challenges, Jess, and maybe you're too accessible."

"But—"

"But nothing. Listen to me. I know what I'm talking about. I dated him, too. Remember?"

"Yeah, I remember."

"So, are you coming over now or what?"

"I'll come. Just remember to be nice to Miranda. She's sensitive."

"I'm always nice," I say, then hang up.

I wrap myself in a robe and wait for Jess and Miranda. Ten minutes later the doorman rings me to get my approval to let my friends up. When I open the door, Miranda is standing behind Jess, looking down at the ground. Miranda is wearing black stretch pants and a huge red sweater that hangs to her knees, as if she's trying to hide her body.

"Hi, Miranda," I say.

She manages a small "Hi," and follows Jess into the condo.

Leading them to my room, I open the door and Mutt, who was locked inside, goes right for poor Miranda's crotch.

"Leave her alone," I say to Mutt, who sniffs loudly then walks out of the room.

I open my closet doors. "Okay, what should I wear?"

I admit I've been blessed with a mom who came up with the *Everyone's a star at Starbucks* campaign. Don't knock it. My entire wardrobe was probably paid with jingles and slogans my mom created. The *Don't Baby Me* slogan for Precious Baby Finger Foods was a big hit along with the jingle *If you know someone who needs someone, call 1-800-Therapy*.

"Are those real Jimmy Choo shoes?" Miranda asks, wide-eyed.

My mom brought them back for me from a fashion show in New York last year. "Yeah. Want to try them on?"

Miranda takes a step back. "Oh, no. I'm so heavy I'd probably break the heel."

"Don't be ridiculous," I say, then grab the shoes and hand them to her. They're slingback and will practically fit anyone. "Just don't let my dog lick them."

Miranda hesitates, then slowly reaches out and takes them from my outstretched hand.

I look over at Jess when Miranda sits on the edge of my bed to take her gym shoes off and put the Jimmy Choos on. She's rummaging through my closet, taking stuff out and laying it over her arm. "I'll give you choices."

"Thanks, Mommy," I say sarcastically.

Jessica rolls her eyes as she lays out the outfit I wore on my last date with Avi. I know it sounds lame, but it's sacred. The memories of that night are attached to that skirt and top. I'm absolutely not wearing it. "Nope. Next."

She holds out a ripped jeans/tight sweater combination. "Nope. Too alternative."

A knock at the door interrupts us. "Amy, it's me." My dad.

When I tell him to come in, he surveys the clothes strewn around the room and Miranda trying to balance in the Choos. "You girls putting on a fashion show? I'll give you money if you'll make Amy clean her room."

"Dad, don't be a dork," I tell him, pushing him out of the room before he embarrasses me more. "I'm going to the youth group meeting tonight. Remember?"

"I remember. But I thought you said it started at four."

"It does."

He checks his watch. "It's five to. You better hurry."

When he's gone, I see the third outfit Jess has picked for me. Dark blue jeans and a simple pink long-sleeve tee with a gold O at the top. While I'm shimmying into the jeans, Miranda stumbles in the Choos over to my nightstand and picks up the picture of Avi. "Is he your boyfriend?"

Jess bites her bottom lip, probably to keep herself from blurting out, "He's her non-boyfriend."

I hesitate before saying, "Kind of."

Miranda looks from the picture of Avi to me. "He's a hottie."

A little part of my heart flips over. Turning around, I finish dressing and say, "I'm ready. Let's go," because I don't want to talk about him. I haven't even written him back and I don't call him at home because I don't want to act like stalker-girlfriend. I'm confused. I hate feeling like this.

When we arrive at the youth group meeting at the synagogue, I'm surprised at the amount of kids here. There must be at least forty kids hanging around the social hall. Some kids I recognize from school, but most I've never seen in my life.

A dark, curly-haired guy with a *kippah* on his head who's probably in his thirties tries to quiet everyone down.

"He's Rabbi Doug, the new assistant rabbi," Jess tells me.

Miranda stays close to Jess's side as we find a vacant place on the floor to sit. It takes a while for everyone else to shut up, but finally all eyes are on Rabbi Doug.

"Is everybody ready to build a *sukkah* for our play?"

Ask me a year ago and I couldn't tell you what a *sukkah* was. Now I know it's a small structure where you invite family and friends to eat the "harvest meal." Normally Jews build a *sukkah* sometime near October for the holiday of Sukkot, but the youth group is putting on a play for the Hebrew school students about the holidays and the *sukkah* is being built tonight.

Rabbi Doug proceeds to have us count off so we're in different groups. I'm in a group with a bunch of kids I don't know. This guy who assigns himself the leader of our group has us meet in the hallway.

A girl with curly black hair and bushy eyebrows is in my group, along with a couple of other girls and a bunch of guys. I sit next to Bushy Brow and give her a small smile.

"I'm Nikki. With an *i*," she says.

Oh, no. Flashbacks of my stepfather, Marc *with a c*, slam into my consciousness. "I'm Amy. With a *y*," I say back.

"Where do you go to school?"

"Chicago Academy. Where do you go?"

At the mention of Chicago Academy, Nikki blinks twice. What is it with people lately? I swear you'd think Chicago Academy was synonymous with School For Brats. "Mather," she replies.

"That's cool."

Nikki isn't über-friendly after I told her I go to Chicago Academy, like she's suddenly wary of me.

Luckily, a cool guy wearing a black hooded sweatshirt sits on the other side of me and starts talking. "What's up? I'm Wes."

"I'm Amy."

"I've never seen you here before," Wes says while checking me out. He's so obvious about it, a guy like that deserves to be played with.

"I'm a youth group virgin," I say.

Instead of being shocked, the guy laughs. "Cool. You might not want to hang with me. I'm so *not* a virgin I might scare you off."

"I go to Chicago Academy," I tell him. "I might scare you off."

Instead of being intimidated, Wes leans forward. "Ooh, one of those rich kids. Is it true your parents host teenage parties with booze and pot?"

"Absolutely," I lie. "What else would we do with all that excess money?"

He laughs and gives me a big, cocky smile. "I like you, Amy."

Rabbi Doug gives us our assignment. "You guys are in charge of hanging the fruit in the *sukkah*. The baskets, hooks, and string are in the back room. Be creative, people."

I follow the rest of the kids to the back room. Wes and I are instant friends, I find out he goes to Mather High, too, and sings in a band called Lickity Split. Nikki is starting to warm up to me, or maybe she likes Wes so she's acting all nicey-nice.

"Do you have a boyfriend?" Wes asks me while we're attempting to string bananas together.

I look over to Jessica's group, working with nails and wood to put up the *sukkah* structure. "Sort of."

"What do you mean by 'sort of'?" Nikki chimes in.

Is it really any of these people's business? "I have a boyfriend, but he's in Israel."

Wes plunges a needle and thread into the skin of the banana. "As in he lives there?"

"Yeah."

"How can he be your boyfriend when he's, like, a million miles away?"

I stop the banana threading. It's like everyone else is putting into words what's been on my mind lately. It's pissing me off. Ever since I talked to my Israeli cousin yesterday, I've been rethinking my relationship with Avi. Obviously I'm not his first priority. Why should he be mine?

Without answering Wes, I wander away from the youth group and stare out at the view of Lake Michigan. The backyard of the synagogue faces the lake, on prime real estate property. I'm sure my stepfather would love to get his hands on this piece of land. I envision myself on the sandy beach below.

An image of Nathan pops into my head, interrupting my thoughts of Avi. Why, I have no clue. It's just...well, Nathan kind of reminds me of Avi. Not his looks, by any means. Avi is drop-dead-oh-my-God gorgeous, the Abercrombie model come to life. Nathan is the opposite. He looks as awkward as he acts and doesn't even care that he's a loner. Avi has a bunch of loyal friends.

Avi and I fell for each other after hating each other for the better part of the summer. In the beginning, we fought every time we came within two feet of each other. When he kissed me, it was as explosive as the fighting and more incredible than any kiss I'd ever had.

I'm sure kissing Nathan would be nothing like kissing Avi.

I put my hands on either side of my head and squeeze my eyes shut. How can I think about kissing Nathan? Eww.

Okay, I'll admit he has unique green eyes. They have little specks of brown and gold in them, and when he looks at me I find myself searching for those specks. A guy like that shouldn't have such cool eyes.

"Hey, Amy, you okay?"

It's Jessica. I don't feel like talking right now, even to my best friend. I'm kind of fine being depressed all by myself. "I'm fine."

"You think the youth group is weak sauce, don't you? I'm sorry I made you—"

"It's not weak sauce."

"Then why are you all mopey?" My best friend rolls her eyes at me, if you can believe it. "Seriously, Amy, you're gonna have to get over Avi. You've been acting like a total recluse lately and it's getting on everyone's nerves, especially mine. Can't you move on? I guarantee Avi's not moping around, making his friends and everyone else around him miserable."

I stand here wide-eyed, not believing for a second Jessica just bitched me out. She's never done this before. We've always supported each other through guys and zits and parents and school. "I guess it's too much to ask for my best friend to support me when I need it the most," I say.

"You know what, Amy? I was thinking the same thing," she says, then stomps back to the *sukkah*-building activity.

What the hell was that all about? I'm too confused to think right now. All I want to do is go home. What's worse is that I'm at the mercy of Jessica because she drove me here.

Stomping back to my group, I plop myself down next to Wes from Lickity Split again.

"Amy, you just sat on a banana," Wes informs me, then bursts out laughing. Nikki and the rest of my group follow. All eyes are watching to see what I'm going to do next.

I could cry—that wouldn't take too much effort. In fact, I can feel a waterfall forming behind my eyelids.

Closing my eyes, my brain focuses on the wet, gushy mush soaking the jeans I spent over a half hour picking out. And on Jessica's tirade. And on my mom's pregnancy. And on Avi and Nathan and my dad's date disaster. And Mutt's insatiable addiction to sniffing everyone's crotch.

In case you haven't noticed, my teenage life is officially ruined.

12

*Rabbi Glassman said he realized he wanted to study to be
a rabbi when he was in high school.
To be honest, I think God chose him to be a rabbi
instead of the other way around.
He's too unbiased and wise to be a regular person.*

Yes, I had to last the rest of the night with wet, sticky banana-encrusted jeans. And no, Jessica and I still aren't talking. Miranda is, though.

"That was so much fun, wasn't it?" Miranda says as we get into Jessica's car at the end of the night. I put down a plastic bag before I sit in the back seat while the engine is warming up.

Jessica grunts and I say, "Yeah. Great fun." I love being laughed at by an entire group of high schoolers and smelling like baby food. Where can I sign up for the next meeting?

"Sorry about your pants," Miranda says from the front passenger seat. "I'm glad you came, though. There's not many kids from CA here."

"We don't necessarily have a huge Jewish population at the Academy," I say, leaning back and hearing the bag under my butt crinkle with every movement I make. Jewish kids probably make up fifteen or twenty percent of the student population at Chicago Academy, and CA isn't the biggest school in Chicago by far.

"They think we're rich snobs," I blurt out.

Miranda turns and faces me while Jessica concentrates on driving us home. "People don't think I'm a snob. They think of me as the fat girl. They think you're a snob because you're pretty and don't smile a lot."

"Smiling is overrated."

Jessica snorts.

Miranda looks animated now. She's going into excited mode. "Smiling takes years off your life. Did you know it takes more muscles to frown than it does to smile?"

"Did you know it takes more energy to talk than to be silent?"

Did I just say that? Oh, man. Miranda bites her lip and turns around, slinking down in the seat. I didn't mean it. I just wanted to stop feeling like I was bombarded with everyone pointing out what's wrong with me.

Jessica stops the car. I think she's so pissed she's going to dump me off the side of the road and order me to get out. But now I realize we're at my building.

Keeping up with the I'm-not-a-good-friend-and-I-don't-smile theme, I open the door to the car and step onto the sidewalk. I'm about to swallow my pride and thank Jess for the ride, but she blurts out, "Close the door."

As soon as I shut the door, Jessica's off like a NASCAR driver.

I feel like the biggest bitch. Maybe I am. Should I feel better that I'm a bitch with a conscience? Because I feel totally wretched.

I stay on the sidewalk for a minute before I turn and walk into the building. I want to smile. I want to be a good friend to Jessica and even Miranda. Miranda doesn't look or dress or act like me, but she's nice and smiles. Does she smile because she's genuinely nice or is she perceived to be nice because she smiles?

Does it even matter?

Exhausted physically and emotionally, I pass our night doorman Jorge who opens the door for me as I head for the elevator bank.

"Did you have a good evening with your friends, Miss Barak?" Jorge asks.

"Not particularly," I answer back.

"Some days are like that, I'm afraid."

"Yeah, some days are crap."

In the elevator, I lean my head against the wall. The doors start to close, until I hear someone stopping the doors from shutting with their hands. Those hands are attached to none other than Nathan.

Nathan enters the elevator in sweats and workout pants. A lady who I've only seen a few times who lives on the fifth floor follows in right behind him.

I close my eyes to block out everything. When we stop on the fifth floor to let the lady out, I open my eyes.

Nathan is staring right at me through his glasses. His eyes are as bright as Kermit the Frog and the gold specks in them are shining in the lights of the elevator. Stupid lights. Stupid elevator. They make my mind think stupid thoughts, like wondering what I could do to make Nathan like me.

He takes a drink from a water bottle he's carrying in his hand. I start breathing heavily, as if my mind is one big mashed potato. I stare at his lips. I've never noticed them before, but now they're shiny from that water.

Nathan hates me, but maybe...

No, I can't.

But he's looking right at me; our eyes are locked. I can't change anything else in my crappy life, but maybe I can change his attitude and animosity toward me.

If I don't try it, I'll never know. I drop my purse on the floor of the elevator and rush toward him, pressing my lips to his. I'm kissing Nathan in the elevator as we ride up from the fifth to fortieth floor, my eyes still locked on his while I'm waiting for some reaction from him.

I get none.

My hands. What should I do with my hands? I place them on his chest, which feels unusually hard for a guy like him, and tilt my head to attempt a more intimate kiss.

Nathan isn't responding. His lips are soft and inviting but he's standing stiffly with his arms at his side. He's not shoving me away from him, but he surely isn't acting like a guy who's being kissed by a girl. His lips are parted slightly against mine, his breath is warm and smells sweet. But he's not all here. He's not into it and I'm the one doing all the work.

When the elevator dings and the doors open, I lift my hands off his chest and lean back.

"Well, that was pleasant," I say as I lift my purse and step out of the elevator.

"For who?" Nathan responds, walking right past me.

We're in the hall on the fortieth floor of the building with nobody else around. Nathan is in front of his door and I'm in front of mine. I look down the hall at him while he fishes for his keys. "For nobody, Nathan. That was a joke. You obviously don't like girls."

He gives a short, cynical laugh. "Whatever you say, Barbie. Did anyone ever tell you you smell like fruit?"

"Stop calling me Barbie!" I yell, ignoring the fruit comment for the moment. Nathan doesn't respond as he opens the door to his condo and slams the door shut behind him.

The door quickly opens to my condo and my dad rushes at me. "What's wrong? Who are you yelling at?"

"Nobody, Dad."

"I heard you yelling. Are you okay?"

"Don't spaz on me. I'm fine," I say, then brush past him.

My dad follows me to my bedroom, my private sanctuary where I go to be alone. "I'm your father. I have a right to spaz. Why are you acting like this? And why do you smell like bananas?"

I give him my famous sneer. "Acting like what?"

"Like you're angry with the world."

"I'm not angry with the world; the world is angry with me. And for your information, I sat on a banana. Now if you'll excuse me, I'd like some privacy so I can change." That gets him to leave pretty quick.

After I shimmy out of my now crusty jeans, I dress in pj's and head down the hall to brush my teeth and scrub my face. With all the stress I'm under, I'm bound to get a zit or two…or twenty. I'm in the bathroom, scrubbing my lips and that kiss away with a washcloth. Back in my room, I look up and see my dad standing in the doorway.

He leans against the door frame. "I admit I'm not used to teenage girl problems. But I'm here to listen."

I can tell he's mentally preparing for some heavy discussion. He's not used to heavy *teenage girl problem* discussions. My dad is such a guy. He needs some feminine influence in his life. "Why don't you want a girlfriend?"

"Because relationships are a time commitment."

I roll my eyes and say, "It's no secret you have commitment problems. Let's just get that out in the open. Are you refusing to date because you're in love with my mom?"

"I'm not talking about this with you."

"Why not? You're obviously not talking about it with anyone else. And if you think by working yourself to death you can hide from the truth, you can't."

"I'm committed to you, Amy. I hardly have time to spend with my own daughter these days, which is killing me inside. How can I add something else to take me away from my family?"

"You call two people a family?"

"Yes."

My poor dad doesn't get it. "What about when I go to college? You'll be all alone while Marc and Mom have more babies together. And what about after you retire? You'll be sitting at home by yourself with nothing to keep you company but a set of dentures and an old, wrinkly body."

The side of his mouth quirks up in amusement. "Thanks for painting the full picture. Consider me officially forewarned of my future fate."

"Great. Now will you go on a date?"

"No. But I'm coming home early tomorrow to spend time with you. After working at Perk Me Up!, I'll take you anywhere you want to go. *Tov?*"

Leave it to my dad to slide in a Hebrew word now and then. "*Tov,*" I say back.

When he leaves my room, I let out a long, frustrated sigh and look over at my cell phone. I was really rude to Miranda tonight in the car. I practically told her to shut up. And I hate fighting with Jessica. Every time we argue I feel sick.

I decide to text Jessica.

Me: You there?
Jess: No.
Me: Want to talk?
Jess: No.
Me: Fine.
Jess: Fine.

Crossing my room to my desk, I take out the CA student directory and dial Miranda's number.

"Hello?"

"Miranda?"

"Yeah."

"It's Amy. Um…I just wanted to say I'm sorry I was kinda rude tonight. I mean, if I hurt your feelings I didn't mean to. It was the banana incident and—"

"And your fight with Jessica," she says, stating the obvious.

"Yeah, that too. Well, I just wanted to apologize."

"Apology accepted."

Phew. One person to check off my list of people pissed with me. "Maybe we could hang out sometime."

I think Miranda just dropped the phone, 'cause I hear this big bang on the other end of the line. She recovers pretty quickly, though. "You really want to hang out with me?"

"Sure. I know you're in pretty much all AP classes and I'm not, but you were really cool tonight."

"Wow. Thanks," Miranda says excitedly. "You're way more popular than me, Amy, but you must know that. I just thought you would think I was lame like the other girls at school…well, except Jessica. Although Jessica and I don't hang out unless it's for the youth group."

Here's the thing about popularity: it's the ones who declare themselves popular who usually get pegged as popular. You've got to know how to talk big and act like you're someone important and people will treat you like you're big and important. My wonderful mother taught me to be who I want to be without making excuses. I admit sometimes I go a bit overboard with my comments and actions, but I have a conscience. I apologize.

Of course it's only to the people who deserve an apology.

I guess you can call me *apologetically selective*. (I think I just made that up, but I like it.)

"Don't you live next door to that new guy from school?" Miranda asks. "He's totally cute."

Ugh! "You mean Nathan?"

I can feel the vibration of excitement over the line. "Yeah. Nathan. He sits in front of me in calculus and has the coolest eyes. Like emeralds."

"Don't waste your breath, Miranda. He's not into girls."

13

From the beginning when the Israelites were slaves to Pharaoh in Egypt to the Nazis' attempt to annihilate the Jewish race, Jews have suffered—but in the end have prevailed and become stronger.
They've even overcome God's anger (Exodus 32:10).
Overcoming obstacles is in my Jewish blood.

"The whole school thinks I'm gay."

I'm standing at my locker, fishing for my U.S. history book. It's in here somewhere. "Did you say something?" I say sweetly to Nathan, still keeping my attention on the books stacked in my locker.

"Amy."

Oh, there it is. I reach out and grab my book, wondering when Mr. Krazinski will spring a pop quiz on us. Maybe I should take the book home tonight and read it.

Nathan grabs my arm, pulling me away from my locker. "Ouch," I say. He's stronger than I'd ever give him credit for, but it doesn't hurt. I rub my arm for effect.

"I didn't hurt you. Yet."

"What do you want from me, Nathan? I've got to get to class and I'm already late."

He's wearing a stark white button-down shirt and pleated navy pants. I'm not even concentrating on his lack of fashion sense because I'm trying not to look at his eyes. I keep thinking about that ludicrous comment Miranda said about emeralds.

"I want you to admit you told the entire school I'm gay."

Leaning back against the lockers while avoiding his eyes, I say, "Listen, Nathan. I didn't tell anyone you're gay. I *may* have said you're not into girls."

"Why, 'cause I'm not into you?"

"That's low, Nathan."

"Oh, I can get lower, Amy. Just try me." He steps forward and straddles both hands on the lockers behind me, locking me in. "Look at me."

I'd like to still keep my gaze on the wall opposite him, but that would be cowardly. I'm anything but a coward. He's tall and close. I can smell spicy cologne radiating off his body. And when I look up, I'm staring straight into his eyes because his glasses have slipped down. I swallow then say, "What's wrong with people thinking you're gay? Jason Hill is gay and he's probably the most popular guy in school—with girls as well as guys."

"If I was, I wouldn't give a shit. But I'm not."

"So tell everyone you're hetero. Just like I have to tell everyone I didn't join a dating service." I shove his arm out of the way and head to class, thinking all the while that his personality does not in any way match his looks. It's like dressing a buffalo up as a hyena. It's just not right.

Jessica is in my U.S. history class. I sit in my usual spot next to her after being grilled by Mr. Krazinski about why I was late. I lied and said it was *a feminine problem* and that quieted him real quick.

Jess looks horrible. I'd be surprised if she took a shower this morning, she looks so disheveled. Her brown hair is frizzed out; she's wearing sweats and no makeup. I don't care if she was insensitive to me last night. I need to find out what's going on. I've been best friends with Jess for twelve years. Our friendship can weather any fight.

I hope.

Now I'm worried. She won't even look in my direction, so I wait until the bell rings to corner her. I swear this school should be called Drama Academy instead of Chicago Academy today.

When the bell rings, Jess grabs her stuff and hurries out of the classroom faster than a jackrabbit being chased by a dog. I push the other students out of my way to catch up with her. I'm hearing curses from guys as I shove past them but all I can think about is my friend in trouble.

I find her in the girls' bathroom. "Jess, I know you're in here. I *saw* you." When I get no answer, I continue. "I admit I've been wrapped up in my own crap and have ignored you, but *please* let's talk about it."

The door to one of the stalls opens. It's Roxanne Jeffries.

With a toss of her red hair and a smirk on her face, she says, "I hear Mitch dumped Jessica for a freshman."

"Shut up, Roxy, or I'll tell people you got implants last summer when you told everyone you went to overnight camp," I hiss.

"You're a bitch," Roxanne says with a huff.

"So I've been told. Now scram. Your perfume is making me ill. Or maybe it's your B.O. that reeks."

Roxanne washes her hands, then storms out of the bathroom.

"You're not a bitch," Jessica's voice bellows from one of the stalls. I can tell from her tone she's been crying. "You're just preoccupied."

"No, I think everyone's right. I'm a bitch because no matter what's going on in my own life, I should never let down my best friend."

Jess pushes open the stall door with bundled-up tissue in her hand. "I'm sorry what I said about you and Avi."

"I'm sorry for not realizing earlier that you're having a crisis. What's up? Is what Roxanne just said true?"

Her eyes get watery and I hand her a paper towel. "Mitch called me before I left for the youth group thing last night. He said he had something important to talk to me about. I tried getting it out of him, but he said we'd just talk later. I asked him if it was good news and he said no."

I bite my bottom lip in fear. "He didn't?"

"Yep. After I got home from the youth group thing I called him. He broke up with me and said he was asking Kailey Pulson to the Valentine's Dance."

My eyebrows furrow in confusion. "Kailey Pulson? Freshman Kailey Pulson?" Kailey Pulson is a total jock girl. I think she rock climbs for fun.

Tears run down Jess's cheeks as she nods. "Now what am I gonna do?"

The bell rings again. I'm late for another class. "I'll figure something out, Jess. They don't call me your best friend for nothing. What we have to do is find us both hot dates for the dance. Leave it to me."

Jess sniffles. "To be honest, right now I don't want to go. The last thing I want to do is see Kailey and Mitch together."

She has a point. As I open the door to the bathroom, I turn back and face my best friend. "Then we'll just hang out, the two of us dateless girls. We'll watch DVDs, order pizza, and gossip all night. Sound good?"

"Thanks, Amy," Jess says.

I got to English class late because of my chitchat with Jess in the bathroom, but Miss Haskell has a sub so it wasn't a big deal. Can it be a sign of good karma coming my way?

At lunch I pay for the salad bar, then search for Mitch. I'm going to find my old boyfriend and give him a piece of my mind. Jessica told me not to. She wants me to leave him alone but I can't.

"Barbie," a male voice says from behind me. I whip around. Of course it's Nathan. Nobody else would have the nerve to call me Barbie. Without saying another word, he pulls me close and starts kissing me.

I mean *really* kissing me. To the point where I drop my food tray and don't even care I've just made a mess on the floor and on my shoes with a mixture of lettuce and vegetables and Thousand Island dressing. Nathan's soft, inviting lips are open to mine and just when I'm about to pull back and yell at him, he snakes his hand around my waist and pulls me closer.

My brain is telling me to pull away even though my lips are as involved as Nathan's are right now. I grab onto Nathan's biceps and attempt to push him away, but he's too strong and I'm not as determined as I want to be.

Nathan is the one to pull back first, after his glasses hit my face and I wince. He turns to the crowd with a huge grin after he pushes his glasses up and says, *"Fine,* I'll go to the Valentine's Dance with you."

Fine? Nothing is *fine* around here.

The cafeteria is in an uproar with cheers from the guys. I'm still in a daze when the lunchroom lady, Gladys, sees the salad mess on the floor and moves us aside with a look of disgust and comments about PDA rules at Chicago Academy.

When my eyes finally focus, I'm still in shock. Nathan tries to help pick up the mess with Gladys, but she shoos him away with a wave of her hand.

Without a word, I walk through the cafeteria and plop myself down at a lunch table next to an open-mouthed Miranda. I know. I never sit at Miranda's table. I just know Miranda and her friends don't gossip like my friends do.

I give her a small smile. Unfortunately Mr. Emerald Eyes follows my lead and sits down next to me.

"Here," he says, shoving a brown bag at me. "It's my lunch. You can have it since you dropped yours."

As if he's a gentleman. Puh*leaze*.

I look over at Jessica, sitting at the popular girls' table. Less than two hours ago I told her I'd stay home for the Valentine's Dance instead of going. She probably thinks I was lying and I'm hooking up with Nathan.

"I'm not hungry." I bark the words at Nathan. In fact, I don't think I could eat all day after that kiss.

14

Okay, I admit it. Nathan surprised me. I would have never guessed the guy would go ahead and do a crazy thing like kiss me in the cafeteria and declare us a Valentine's Dance couple. Now all the kids at school are whispering about us behind my back, in front of my back, and all around me. They're waiting with bated breath for another Amy/Nathan spotting.

I'm not gonna let that happen.

So after school I take a cab home instead of waiting for the bus. If Nathan has no problems kissing me in front of half of the student body, what other stunt is he going to pull on the bus ride home?

After I let Mutt do his duty, I walk over to Perk Me

Up! The rich smells coming from the café immediately make me feel energized and lift my spirits. I don't even need to consume the coffee in order to get the caffeine fix.

Marla hands me an apron and I'm immediately into Perk Me Up! employee mode. I clean off tables, start taking orders, and try to keep a big bright smile on my face. *Show teeth when you smile*, Marla told me last week. Yeah, I'm trying.

My toothy smile fades when Nathan walks in to the café. He has his backpack slung over his shoulder and I didn't notice it before, but he's got splotches of Thousand Island dressing on his white shirt. I don't think those stains are going to come out.

"I'm sorry," he says when he reaches the register. Unfortunately nobody else is in line behind him.

Marla stands beside me, watching and listening.

I ignore Nathan's apology and instead say to him, "Welcome to Perk Me Up! Can I take your order, sir?"

"Come on, Barbie. You kissed me yesterday. Why am I the villain for kissing you today?"

"You kissed him?" Marla asks.

I turn to her. "Only because I wanted him to stop hating me."

Marla's eyebrows furrow in fascination. "You kiss people who hate you?"

"I don't hate her," Nathan chimes in.

"Oh, really?" I say sarcastically, putting my hands on my hips. "Then why do you keep calling me Barbie? And why didn't you kiss me back yesterday when we were in the elevator, but today you have no problem making out with me with the entire school watching?"

"It was to prove a point."

"To prove you're not gay? Listen, you're not cute enough to be gay."

Nathan laughs. "Are you kidding me? You are the most stereotypical, insensitive, and obnoxious girl I've ever met."

"I take offense to that," I say, then cross my arms in front of my chest.

"Me, too," Marla interjects. "Amy's rough around the edges, but she's as good as gold."

"Oh, you're so sweet, Marla," I say, then hug her.

Nathan points to me. "She thinks I'm a dork because I wear old clothes and have glasses."

"Well, he thinks I'm a bitch because I say out loud what everyone else is thinking."

"You know what *I* think?" Marla says, stepping closer to the counter.

Nathan and I say, "What?" in unison.

"I think you two like each other."

I roll my eyes while Nathan does a shiver as if the thought of liking me grosses him out.

"Nope," he says.

"Not *at all*," I say. "Besides, I have Avi. And he's got Bucky."

"Bicky."

"Whatever."

"Yep," Marla says, then saunters to the supply room

like she knows what's going on. "You guys definitely like each other."

Nathan starts to laugh.

"It's not funny," I say. More customers come into the café, so it's my chance to say to Nathan, "Please order or step aside so I can wait on someone else."

"I'll have a medium green tea with ice, no sweetener," he says, diverting my attention back to him.

Figures he'd order something so plain.

After I take his money and turn around to make his boring drink, Nathan says so only I can hear, "Don't spit in it."

As if I would. Puh*leaze*.

I hand his drink to him and focus my attention on the other customers.

The hour goes by fast. Making drinks, cleaning off the tables, and ignoring Nathan typing away in the computer corner is exhausting, though. I sigh in relief when my dad walks through the door to pick me up.

My dad has already changed clothes from work. He's wearing dark jeans and a black long-sleeve tee. I've convinced him to grow his hair out a bit, so he resembles a cuter and cooler dad but he's still got about two months to go before he can get a good style going.

"Hey, *Aba*," I greet him.

Out of the corner of my eye I swear I see Nathan watching us.

"How was school today?" my dad asks.

I look over at Nathan. Now he's pretending to read the computer screen, but I know he's not reading a damn thing. He's wondering if I'll tell my dad what happened in the cafeteria. "Nothing much. What about you?"

My dad kisses the top of my head. "Just preparing for a presentation in D.C. You ready to go?"

"Yep."

"Great. Where to?"

I grab my dad's elbow and journey into the cold outside air. "Follow me," I say, leading him down State Street.

I lean into my dad to try and soak up some of the warmth of his strong commando arm. "I'm sorry I yelled at you yesterday," I say. "I just want you to be happy."

"I'm sorry, too. You didn't make any more dates for me, did you?"

"Here we are," I tell him as we turn down artsy Oak Street with the designer shops and upscale salons. I pull him into the first building we come to, a place called Sheer-Ahz. I purposely leave out the speed-dating thing I signed him up for at the last minute.

"You're getting a haircut?" he asks when he realizes Sheer-Ahz is a salon.

"Nope."

He halts his steps abruptly. "Then why the salon?"

I look up at him and smile widely as if he was a customer at Perk Me Up! "We're getting manicures."

"You mean *you're* getting a manicure."

"Nope. You heard me right the first time, *Aba*."

"Men don't get manicures."

"Come, on. Haven't you heard of metrosexual men?"

My dad shakes his head. "No. And I'm sure I don't want to be one."

"Didn't you say I could pick what we do tonight?"

"Yes, but—"

I turn to my dad, one of the few people who takes my crap and loves me despite it. Maybe even more because of it. My dad pretends he's not afraid of anything, but I've just uncovered his weakness…getting his nails trimmed and shaped. Give me a break. "This is what *I* want to do. My nails are all dry and cracked. Think of it as daddy/daughter bonding time."

"Can't we bond by playing indoor soccer or something like that?" he says.

"I don't do soccer. I do manicures." I pull all six feet of him up to the front desk. "We have appointments for two manicures," I inform the lady. "For Amy and Ron Barak."

She doesn't flinch as she punches our names in the computer, writes something on two tickets, and hands them to us. "Feel free to have refreshments in the meditation room while you're waiting."

My dad turns to me and says, "Did she just say meditation room?" in his deep, manly voice. I swear he's making it sound deeper than usual.

Once inside the white silk-draped room with scented candles and soft music, he looks nervous. I don't think a retired Israeli commando has ever been in a place like this. He'd probably look more at home in the desert. Or in a war zone.

There are no other guys in the room, just a lady in

a terry cloth robe. I bet she's got nothing on underneath. She's reading one of the complimentary magazines and doesn't pay any attention to us.

"Sit down," I tell my dad while I sink into the plushy, soft, cream-colored chair and breathe to the rhythm of the slow music.

"I'd rather stand," he says tersely.

My eyes close as my mind drifts. "Suit yourself."

After a few minutes, two women dressed in long, white coats call out, "Ron and Amy Barak."

"That's us," he says, then clasps his hands together and rubs them back and forth. The sound is making me cringe and everyone is staring at him. Real smooth, Dad.

When we're sitting down next to each other, the nail technician takes my dad's hand and places it in a small container of soapy water.

"I don't want a color," he tells the woman right away.

I want to groan. Does he honestly think they're going to make his nails a brilliant red or fuchsia pink? "*Aba*, guys get clear. Or just a buff." Duh.

"Oh. Okay…I think."

Seriously, take a guy out of his element and he gets all confused and insecure. My own nail technician, Sue, is expertly massaging my wrists, palms, and hands as they turn to Jell-O under her skilled touch.

"My daughter made me come here," my dad tells the women, but he says it loud enough so everyone in the small salon can hear him. *Go, manly man! Yes, tell all women you a strong warrior man.* Spare me.

"*Aba*, you've got calluses and your skin is all dry and cracked. I swear you look like a dinosaur. Right, Sue? Just look at his paws."

Sue is extremely non-committal as she glances at my dad's hands. She smiles sweetly at him, then continues to work magic with my fingers.

I can tell when my dad's nail tech starts his own hand massage. His shoulders, for the first time since we got here, slump into relaxation mode.

His hair has curled from the dampness in the air, making him look younger and vulnerable. I wonder if he was ever insecure. As a teen did he go through an awkward stage or was he hard and manly and confident since the day he was born?

My dad looks Middle Eastern with his dark olive complexion, dark features, and strong chiseled nose. If he was a stranger, I wouldn't immediately think he was Jewish, though. I wonder if he ever wanted to be something other than what he is.

Because I never thought I'd want to be any religion, but now I feel different. Being Jewish isn't a choice; it's a part of me. A part I just discovered, but it's significant in any case.

"After I convert I want a bat mitzvah," I tell my dad, bringing him to attention.

"With a big party?" he asks.

Thinking about it more, I decide I don't want a big shindig. "I'd just like Jessica and a few other friends to come over afterward. And Mom and Marc. You know, if it's okay with you."

"It's fine. In fact, it's great."

He's watching intently as his cuticles are cut and fortified and his nails are shaped. I think he's enjoying it as much as I am, but I'm not sure if my "manly man" dad will admit it.

I pick a French manicure while he picks out a sheer, almost invisible bottle of polish.

When we're done, the nail techs lead us into the drying area and instruct us to place our wet nails under ultra-violet lights to get them to dry fast.

I put my hands under the lights while my dad picks up his ultra-violet light machine and examines it.

"Put that down before you get us in trouble," I whisper.

"Before I stick my hands under something, I'd like to know exactly what it is. Don't be so trusting, Amy," he advises, going into Homeland Security mode.

I chuckle. "Yeah, the nail technicians are the enemy. Be afraid. Be *very* afraid."

He puts the machine down but still doesn't stick his hands underneath the fluorescent blue light. "Let's talk about Avi," he says, still refusing to put his hands under the light.

"Why?"

He shrugs. "I just want to know if you're still an item."

"Dad, the word 'item' went out in the seventies but yes, I still like him. I mean, we haven't been able to see each other but I'm hoping in the summer when we go back to Israel he'll get time off." I take a sideways look at my dad. "You know he's my *non-boyfriend*, right?"

"What exactly does that mean?" he asks. "I've heard you and Jessica using the phrase, but I don't get it."

I check my nails to see if they're still tacky and need more ultra-violet rays but they're as dry as my stepdad's liquor cabinet. I hop off the stool I've been sitting on, trying to explain the relationship label Avi wanted. "It means we can see other people because we obviously can't physically be together. There's no commitment. We're casual, great friends. Get it?"

He nods. "Got it."

"Speaking of casual friends, I have a surprise for you."

"It's not another online date, is it?"

"Oh, no," I say, shaking my head vigorously. "It's a bunch of dates. Tonight. Speed dating at the Blues Bar on Chicago Avenue and you have to be there in fifteen minutes. Don't worry about impressing anyone. You only have three minutes for each date. It's all about making a connection."

15

Israel is tiny, yet everyone fights over it.
I guess it's true that the biggest and best things come in
small packages.

My manipulation skills obviously need help, because my dad refused to even step one foot inside the bar for the speed dating night.

Standing in front of the bar, I wait until the bouncer is preoccupied and slink inside without him noticing.

"He's not coming?" Marla is there, wearing a black scooped-neck dress. She got so excited when I told her about the speed dating she decided to sign up, too. She and my dad aren't compatible. She's into mushy romantic guys and my dad is…well, he's not. He's Israeli.

I walk up to the guy running the program, a balding guy with a ring of red hair around his scalp. He's got a nametag on his chest with the word LARRY in big black letters. "My dad couldn't make it," I tell Larry, looking over his notes. The bar is crowded. I refuse to cancel my dad's reservation to date twenty women in an hour and a half.

Larry looks up at me. "Your dad?"

"Yeah, I kind of signed him up."

"You can't do that. Did you read the rules?" The guy doesn't even question what a seventeen-year-old is doing in a bar in the first place.

Umm... "I'm not a rule kind of person."

"What's his name?"

"Ron...Ron Barak."

My mouth opens wide as he takes a big red pen and crosses off my dad's name from the list.

"You can't do that!" I say, totally upset now. I paid thirty-five dollars to sign my dad up for the speed dating night. Okay, to be completely honest Marla paid and I'm working it off. It's a little side business arrangement I made with her.

Marla takes a seat next to Larry and makes her lips all pouty. "Is there any way you could help her out?"

The guy shrugs. "What do you want me to do?"

Marla looks to me for an answer.

"Let me go on the dates in my dad's place." I admit it isn't the most brilliant idea, but it does have potential. If I could find the perfect woman for him, screen her personally...

Before the guy comes to his senses, I pull a nametag and scorecard off the table.

"Women, please sit at your assigned places. Men, you'll

go around to each woman, marking off either a 'yes' or a 'no' on the card. Women, you'll do the same for the men. Just write their number on your card and mark it with a 'yes' or 'no.' If you get two matching 'yes' marks, we'll e-mail you each other's contact information. Everyone got it?"

Nope. But I can't say anything because I'll be kicked out of this ridiculous shenanigan. Right now I'm not blaming my dad. I'm so nervous, as if I'm going to be judged for my looks and brains and...

"Start!"

I head to the only open seat in the place. I'm sitting across from a woman with the name Dru on her nametag. She looks really confused. It takes me a minute to explain myself. "Hi, I'm Amy. My dad was supposed to be here, but couldn't make it. Well, actually he didn't want to come. It's kind of a long story, but ultimately I'm looking for a wife for my dad. What kinds of qualifications do you—"

"Switch!"

Before I finish my question, I'm being rushed out of the chair. I take another empty seat and find myself across from another single, confused woman. She's looking a little old to be set up with my dad, and her gray roots need to be touched up. "How old are you?" I ask.

"Forty."

"Have you tried nighttime moisturizing face cream?"

"I beg your pardon? This is a speed dating function, not a cosmetic consultation."

"I know. I'm trying to find a woman for my dad, but—"

Oops, the lady is raising her hand, getting the attention of the organizers. I crane my neck to find Marla deep in conversation with a guy at the other end of the bar. At least one of us is having luck tonight.

"Switch!"

Larry stands over my chair. "Miss, you can't be here. This is a private function for adults only."

I stand up, defeated. "I'm going, I'm going," I say, then give a little wave to Marla and head outside.

In our condo, my dad is sitting at his desk, working.

"I'll have you know I went on two three-minute dates for you."

"How were they?"

"Terrible. You know how they say there's a pot for every lid? I think you've got a pot in the shape of a trapezoid."

"Is that bad?" he asks.

To be honest, the jury's out on that one. Being unique and different is good. But I suspect there's a fine line between being unique and needing major therapy.

16

Some people will think differently of me
because I'm Jewish.
Some people will call me names because I'm Jewish.
Some people will hate me because I'm Jewish.
Should I ignore them or confront them?

Before school the next day, I spot Mitch by his locker.

"You don't break up with someone right before the Valentine's Dance," I tell him. "It's rude."

He furrows his bushy eyebrows, which at one time I thought made him look rugged and adorable. "What do you want me to say?" he says, then closes his locker and walks away from me.

Why can girls be strong enough to confront boys with issues, but boys can't do the same? They make asinine statements and run away. I'm going to make a generalized statement about boys, so brace yourself: *Boys have an aversion to confrontation.* (And commitment, but that's a whole different story.)

But I am persistent. Catching up with Mitch, I tap him on the back and say as we're walking, "You hurt Jessica. That wasn't cool."

Mitch stops, but his curly hair is still bouncing up and down on his head. "Lay off, Amy. I liked you, then I stopped liking you and fell for Jessica. Now I like someone else."

"Can't you commit to someone?"

"Yeah, while I like 'em. When it's over, it's done. I'm a teenage guy. I can afford to be picky."

I want to slap him.

While I'm still contemplating his egotistic statement, he leaves me in the hallway standing amongst the student body. How many of these teens are picky? Nathan told Marla I don't like him because he wears old clothes and has glasses.

That's not why.

I have the sudden urge to share with Nathan why I hate him. It's not that I'm picky, or rude, or think of myself as too good to be friends with him.

"Earth to Amy."

I blink out of my daydreaming. Cami and Raine are standing in front of me, waving their arms in front of my face. "Welcome back to reality," Cami says, laughing.

"What's on the menu for lunch?" I ask, trying to forget about Mitch and what he just told me. Besides, on Mondays sometimes they surprise us with Uno's pizza. (Another high carb food, I know…but just as worth it as sushi.)

"Forget lunch. Tell us about that Nathan guy and you going to the Valentine's Dance. Everyone's talking about it, if you haven't noticed. They're saying you've gone geek on us. First you kiss the guy in the lunchroom and then you sit at Miranda's table. What's gotten into you?"

I think about how cool Miranda was after I was rude and how quickly she took my apology without making me feel bad. She could have bitched me out, but she didn't. "Miranda's not so bad."

Raine puts her manicured hands up. "She smells like Swiss cheese, Amy. You'd think that big Jewish honker of hers would notice it."

And there it is. My first time since going through conversion someone saying a derogatory remark to me about Jews. More than derogatory. Racist, really. My heart is pounding faster and I feel my throat start to constrict. I'm getting a sick feeling in the pit of my stomach.

"*I'm* Jewish," I say, ready to defend my people even if it costs me popularity-wise. And let me tell you, being unpopular at Chicago Academy is like being a lone rabbit surrounded by a roomful of hunting dogs. Or wolves.

"Yeah, but not really. You're only half Jewish," Raine says, not getting it.

Eww. Half. Like I can never be whole because my mom isn't Jewish? Wrong. "Um, I gotta disagree with you there, Raine. I'm all Jew. If you want to start throwing around Jewish jokes or insults, it's not gonna fly with me."

Raine looks like she's smelling some bad cheese right about now. "Lighten up, Amy."

"Don't tell me to lighten up when you insult my people," I say.

"I insulted Miranda Cohen, Amy. Not you. Not the

entire Jewish population or *your people*. Geez," she says, then rolls her eyes.

I desperately want to walk away, to back down and remove myself from the situation like Mitch did to me. But I don't. Because I want Raine to know, or anyone else who wants to fling around Jewish insults, that it's not okay. It hurts. I can't even describe how much her words cut right through me, even though I know she doesn't realize it.

My heartbeat somewhat gets back to normal when Raine turns and walks away in a huff.

I turn to Cami, who's pretending to check in her book bag for something. I can tell she's just shuffling around stuff. "I'm not mad at you," I tell Cami.

Cami looks up. "That was intense."

"It wasn't meant to be."

So now we're just standing here and I have to say something to break the silence. "You headed for the cafeteria?"

Cami hesitates before saying, "Nope. I have to go to the Resource Lab first. I'll meet up with you later."

Yeah, sure. "Whatever," I say, as if I don't care.

Walking into the cafeteria, I survey my surroundings. Raine is already here; she's talking with a couple of other girls with their heads together in obvious gossip-mode. Did I say gossip was underrated? Well, now that I'm on the other end of the Gossip Trail I'm not so happy about it. Payback sucks.

I'm standing in line, picking out food. Yesterday was a disaster with Nathan's kiss. Now Raine is gossiping about me being Jewish. I'm sure she's twisting the story around to make me look bad. I'm determined to avoid drawing attention to myself.

Oh, no. Nathan just walked in the room. He's about six people behind me in the cafeteria line. He's talking to Kyle. Better to know where he is so I'm not given another surprise kiss without being prepared for it.

Today I don't take a salad, especially because the lunchroom lady Gladys is watching me like a hawk. I order a turkey sandwich on sourdough bread, freshly made at the deli counter, and scan the lunchroom tables.

Here's where life gets tricky.

The lunchroom. Where the students classify and separate themselves like little granola clusters. Usually I'm attached to Jessica. Wherever she sits, I sit. Right now she's at the condiment counter, squirting ketchup into a little white cup for her fries. She has no clue Raine is talking about how she made fun of Miranda's Jewish nose.

Miranda is sitting with her usual cluster. They are not all Jewish. The thing they have in common is they all need fashion advice. They're also straight A students. Miranda waves over to me, and I wave back. She probably thinks I'm going to sit at her table like yesterday.

Jess sits in Raine's cluster before I can get her attention.

Looking back, Nathan is at the cashier about to pay for his two slices of pizza and bottle of Arizona Iced Tea.

Okay, time to make a decision. Cluster with Jessica and Raine, where I usually sit. Or sit with Miranda and her friends again. No time to dawdle, Amy. Popular girls don't dawdle.

As if I'm a programmed robot, I sit with my usual friends. I feel like a traitor, although when I glance over at Miranda, she's in a heated conversation with someone else and doesn't even notice I've chosen the popular girls who know what DKNY means, instead of her table, where they're probably discussing $E=MC^2$.

When I take a seat next to Jessica, the table gets super quiet. Jess is confused.

"So, what's with you and the new guy Nathan?" Roxanne asks with a snicker. "You two put on a pretty good show yesterday. Any chance for a repeat performance?"

I take a bite of my turkey sandwich so I don't have to answer right away. I need time to think of a response, although I'm usually quick-witted.

Just as I'm swallowing my first bite, I hear Nathan's voice behind me. "Can I squeeze in?"

I look up at Nathan and want to say "No" because everyone is expecting us to start making out. Why doesn't he go sit with Kyle and his buddies? Or with the geeks at the geek table?

Jessica makes everyone move down so he can sit next to me. Ugh, all eyes are on us. I do want to talk to Nathan, but in private without being surrounded and stared at by the cluster.

"So, I hear you guys are going to the Valentine's Dance," Roxanne says, her beady eyes focusing on my reaction. "Are you two, like, dating?"

I feel like the entire lunchroom is listening to my response.

"Oh, yeah," I say. "Didn't you know? It was love at first sight. Right, Nathan?"

It's either going to be me and Nathan against Roxanne and the rest of the bunch, or me against everyone.

I turn my head and look at Nathan, sitting beside me. The fluorescent lights of the cafeteria are reflected in his glasses, so I can't see his eyes. But those circular frames are definitely directed at me. "Yeah, right," he says. "I guess it's true. Opposites attract."

I chow on another bite of my sandwich, staring down at my food so I don't have to talk.

But I do see Nathan's fingers, reaching for his pizza. Within three minutes he's picking up the second piece. It's probably a world record in pizza eating. By the time he's done with his second slice, students are still entering the cafeteria.

One gulp of iced tea and he's done. I'm still trying to choke down my sandwich.

Nathan murmurs something to me in my ear that I can't understand, and leaves.

"What did he say?" Jess asks, obviously confused. She knows Nathan and I aren't even friends. Okay, we did kiss. But it was for show. I wasn't even a willing participant the second time.

"No idea," I mumble, then take another bite.

After school, Jess catches up to me on the way to the bus stop.

"Amy," she says. "I don't get it. You think Nathan is a dork—don't even argue with me because I know you better than your own mom does. Then you kiss him in front of the entire school while you're still hung up on Avi. Raine is telling everyone you've gone wacko on her. It doesn't make sense."

"Life doesn't make sense, Jess. Do you hate me?"

"Why would I hate you? I may not understand you. I may get mad at you. But I could never hate you."

Nathan is walking toward us, his uptight gait is so dorky I want to wince. I swear the guy needs a lesson in loosening up and being crazy. He probably dances like a sixty-year-old.

Avi is an amazing dancer. I remember in Israel last summer he was dancing with a girl and I got jealous so I picked a guy at random and pulled him out on the dance floor. Biggest mistake. Let's just say the end result almost had me arrested by the Israeli police.

When Nathan reaches us, Jessica walks to the bus stop to give us privacy. She's such a good friend. Totally mistaken about the situation between me and Nathan, but her heart is in the right place.

I tap Nathan on his elbow. "We need to talk."

"Why? You want to kiss again?"

"And have your glasses whack me in the face again? I don't think so. I want to talk. The kind of talking where lips don't touch."

"Sorry. No can do."

The bus is turning the corner. "Well, we can't keep pretending to be dating."

"Sure we can," he says, putting his arm around me and leading me to the back so we sit with everyone else.

I shrug his arm off.

When we get to our stop, we climb off the bus and he puts his arm around my shoulders again as if we're a real couple. Before I can shrug him off again, I look up. My heart slams into my chest and I almost fall backward.

Standing at the front of my building, like an Abercrombie model posing without even meaning to, is Avi.

And he's watching me walk toward him with Nathan's arm around me. I'm too shocked to ask Avi how he got here, why he's here, how long he's going to stay, or if he still cares about me.

"Avi," I say softly when we get closer to him. I swear I'm still in a trance when I add, "What are you doing here?"

"Who's this guy?" he answers back.

17

> *If God made the world in six days (Genesis 2:2),*
> *surely I can make sense of my life in seven.*

I shrug Nathan's arm off me. He drops it from my shoulders, but still stands next to me. What, is Nathan waiting for a formal introduction? I'm not prepared to give it, even when I find myself saying, "Avi, this is Nathan. Nathan, this is my…this is Avi."

It was a big deal to Avi that we didn't label ourselves boyfriend and girlfriend, with him in the Israeli army for the next three years. As much as my mind agreed with it, my heart didn't. My ego didn't, either. So I end up telling everyone he's my non-boyfriend. Let them decide what it means.

I look at Avi; his stance is stiff and his jaw is tight. He's always been guarded and tough, and I can feel he's already putting up an invisible thick wall between us, ready to shut me out. And he's been with me less than two minutes.

Which actually pisses me off because he was the one who didn't want to be official boyfriend and girlfriend. I did.

I watch as Avi reaches out to shake Nathan's hand. They're so opposite. Avi is the model type and Nathan is this all-American boy-next-door (who needs a major makeover). They give one hard "shake and release" with their hands.

"I got time off," Avi says. "For a week. Surprise, surprise."

A week. I have a week with him. A part of me is giddy beyond belief that I'll have seven days to spend with him and the other half is mad because it's just a tease. Just when I'm ready to move on in my life, he shows up and messes it all back up.

Nathan is still standing beside me, watching me with those stupid emerald eyes. "Catch you later, Amy," he says, then opens the door to our building.

He doesn't call me Barbie. Why that fact should stick in my brain is beyond me.

"Don't you have a suitcase?" I ask Avi.

"I left my duffle with the security guy inside." He puts his hands in his jeans pockets and looks away from me. "This was a bad idea, Amy. I thought…well, screw what I thought. I have a friend at Northwestern I can stay with."

A gust of Chicago wind rushes through the street and chills me to the bone. "You shouldn't have surprised me. I hate surprises. Although I probably should have told you that a long time ago. But now that you know, don't do it again."

Avi's eyebrow quirks up. "I told your dad," he says. His voice is smooth and reminds me of dark chocolate milk.

"Great. My dad knows more about my boyf—about you than I do."

Ah, it all makes sense now, why my dad asked me how I felt about Avi when we had our manicures.

"I thought you'd want me to come."

"I do, Avi," I say, but I can tell by the way he's standing stiff he doesn't believe me.

Right now is the awkward stage. I mean, really, we haven't even touched or hugged or really, *really* looked at each other yet. I can tell him how much I've missed him until I'm blue in the face, though I'm already blue in the face because I'm freezing my ass off out here.

"Let's talk up in my condo, okay?"

He nods and follows my lead. The doorman gives Avi his huge, army green duffle as we pass.

In the elevator, Avi looks straight ahead while I stand behind him. I can't believe he's actually here, in America, in Chicago, in my elevator!

I have so many questions running through my head, number one being why is he here? I thought he'd be in training until February.

Glancing at him, I analyze the differences a few months can make. Wow, he looks taller and more muscular than he did last summer—he's obviously been working out. And I swear he's standing straighter and has a determined look to him that I don't remember. Raw confidence.

A commando in the making.

Although there's a caged animal energy radiating from him, as though being in an elevator is making him claustrophobic.

The door to the elevator opens and I lead him to my condo. Mutt greets us with energetic "Args!" and a tail wagging so hard I think it'll fall off if he gets any more excited.

Avi's eyes go wide. "He's *gadol*...big," he says in Hebrew and English as he leans over to pet Mutt. When Mutt goes for his crotch, Avi says in a calm, deep voice, "*Die.*"

"That's not nice to say to my dog," I say. Maybe Avi's not the guy I once thought he was. Telling my dog to die is not my idea of being cool.

Avi stands up tall. "*Die* means 'stop' in Hebrew, Amy. As in 'that's enough; I don't want your nose in my balls.' That okay with you?"

Oh, no. Things are not going well at all. "Yeah," I say sheepishly. "That's fine."

Mutt scratches the door and noses the leash. I wish Mutt would wait, but if you gotta go, you gotta go no matter if you're human or animal.

"I need to take him out or he'll pee on the floor," I say.

Avi drops his duffle and says, "I'll go with you."

The problem is we need to talk honestly and openly (at the dog park that's not going to happen). I don't want to alienate Avi more than I already have. "That's okay. It'll just take me a minute. I mean, it'll just take Mutt a minute. Wait here, okay?"

He nods. "Fine."

I hurry and clip Mutt's leash to his collar. In the elevator, Mutt looks up at me with his puppy dog eyes that are so expressive sometimes I think there's a human soul inside all of that fur. "Avi's here," I tell him. "And it's awkward. What can I do to make it all better?"

Mutt looks up at me, sticks his tongue out, and pants like a…like a dog who wants to pee.

No answers from this genius dog.

At the dog park, I unclip the leash when we're fenced inside the park. My mind isn't on Mutt. It's on Avi. I contemplate what I'm going to say to him when I get back upstairs.

Do I tell him I kissed Nathan…twice?

It didn't mean anything, and yet I did participate. But how much participating do you have to do before it can really be labeled cheating?

Although how can I cheat on someone who I'm not even officially dating? Does the label of "dating" matter, or is it the feelings in your heart that takes precedence? Oh, man, I am so screwed up. Can my life get any worse?

As if on cue, I hear screaming and a ruckus coming from the other end of the dog park. I turn around and my eyes go wide when I see Mutt humping another dog.

He's usually humping another male dog, showing him who's the boss.

But not this time.

My mutt Mutt is humping Princess. Mr. Obermeyer's prized purebread Princess.

And he is going at it but good. Oh, shit.

When I run over, Mr. Obermeyer is screaming at me, "Get your dog off her!"

I swallow, hard. "What…what do you want me to do?"

In a state of panic, I catch Mitch watching the whole obscene scene and laughing. Most of the other people have their mouths wide open in horror because everyone knows to keep their dog away from Princess and Mr. Obermeyer.

I start yelling words to make Mutt leave Princess alone. "Mutt, come! Treat! No! Get off! Leave her alone! *DIE!*" Yeah, even that last word Avi just taught me didn't work.

Now all I want to do is DIE.

"Do *something*, besides give commands your dog doesn't follow," Mr. Obermeyer yells. "Hurry!"

I take a step toward the two dogs in a romantic dance. "Get off Princess," I growl through clenched teeth. "She's not your type."

Mutt obviously has selective hearing.

When I move closer, I'm getting queasy. I'm not an all-natural-comfortable-in-nature kind of person. Interrupting two dogs in the middle of a very private moment in a very public setting is not my thing and never will be.

Taking a deep breath and bracing myself for humiliation, I step behind Mutt and wrap my arms across his middle. And pull. And pull. But Mutt refuses to let go. Damn.

As soon as I release my grip and give up, Mutt bounds away from Princess as if the entire thing was no big deal.

Mr. Obermeyer runs over to his bitch. "He's tainted her womb."

"Mr. Obermeyer, she's just a dog."

The old man blinks in shock and I think he just turned a paler shade of white, if it was possible. "Princess is a state champion in obedience."

"Obviously," I mutter.

Mr. Obermeyer regards the crowd, still gathered around. "Someone call the police."

I can just see me being dragged to jail because my dog humped a prized poodle named Princess. "Mr. Obermeyer...please."

"Who's going to pay for the veterinary costs for this fiasco? She's in heat and was supposed to be bred with a stud. Now she'll have a litter of mutts instead of purebreds. It's all because you can't control your *animal*."

The old man looks like he's about to have a coronary and his wrinkles threaten to crease further into his waxy skin. "I'm sorry," I say, trying to break the tension while thinking the only stud around here is my mutt.

Mr. Obermeyer holds his hands up. "Sorry?" he says. "How is your 'sorry' going to change the situation?"

It can't. "I don't know."

"If he's not a purebred, your responsibility is to have him fixed." Pursing his lips together, Mr. Obermeyer stalks off with Princess strutting beside him.

I don't care if Mutt isn't a purebred. He's mine. And

Avi gave him to me, which makes him more valuable than any purebred.

Oh, no! Avi.

I run over to Mutt and clasp the leash on him. I walk back home, but stay a safe distance behind Mr. Obermeyer and his bitch, waiting long enough for them to reach the condo before I venture into the elevator with my stud.

I find Avi sitting on our couch, his elbows resting on his knees and his hands clasped together.

"Sorry it took so long," I say, releasing Mutt and hanging the leash back on the hook. "There was kind of a commotion at the dog park." I look over at Mutt, who is now stretched out on his back on the floor looking more relaxed and content than I've ever seen him.

What am I going to tell my dad about Princess and Mutt?

"I thought you ditched me," Avi says, the side of his mouth quirked up. "Amy, the more I'm here, the more I realize this was a bad idea."

I step around the couch and sit next to him. "Don't say that. There's just a lot going on right now."

His midnight eyes are so different from Nathan's. They're brooding, just like my dad's. I can tell he's been through a lot just by staring into them. He's worried about something but he's trying not to show it.

"How's the Israeli army?" I ask.

"*Sababa*," he says.

"What's *sababa*?"

"It means 'cool, awesome, no problem.'" He talks in

that deep, dark voice of his that can melt my own invisible walls I've built around myself.

"You look bigger and more muscular than this summer." Most American guys I know don't look as serious or manly at eighteen years old.

"Survival training will do that to a guy."

I nod. Survival training. My survival training consists of running to the racks at Neiman Marcus on the opening day of their winter blowout sale. It doesn't tone my muscles, but it definitely does hone my skills in sniffing out the best deals before anyone else can get to them. Kinda different than being stuck in a desert with a gun as your only companion. Although Neiman Marcus can be considered a battleground on those winter blowout days.

"I missed you," I say. I omit the fact that I've thought about him every single day since I came back from my trip to Israel. I also fail to mention that I've been having doubts about our relationship...or non-relationship, as it might be. And even though I'm totally blown away with seeing him again, I don't want to be a "friend with benefits." I want more.

Does he? And where does Nathan fit into all of this?

Ugh, I'm an emotional mess.

Avi's hand reaches out to mine. As he takes hold of it, the warmth and comfort I've been missing since the summer comes rushing back to me. His other hand touches my shoulder and slowly moves up, caressing my neck and cheek. I lean my cheek into his palm, the warmth of it drawing me in.

"I missed you, too," he says.

I tentatively lick my lips, scared for this first kiss that will tell both of us where we stand in this relationship. We've got a lot to live up to. Our summer makeout sessions were sensual and emotional and made me feel drugged without any chemicals or alcohol.

He leans forward, watching me. His eyes are fixed on mine. "I shouldn't want you so bad," he says, then his full lips capture mine.

It starts off like before. He brushes his lips over mine as if he's painting them…memorizing the shape and softness. I'm totally getting into it, but then my mind wanders. I have no clue why. Thoughts of Nathan, and Mutt's fiasco, and my mom's pregnancy, and the dates I keep bungling and…

When Avi's tongue reaches for mine, the events of the day are swirling in my head. And I have this nagging feeling I'm forgetting something really important, but I can't remember what. Especially while Avi's trying to take our kisses to the next level, concentrating is impossible.

I lean back and break the kiss.

Those beautiful brooding eyes are staring back at me. "What's going on? Is it that guy? Just *tell* me," he says.

Now I remember! With his lips on mine I couldn't think, but now my brain starts to function again. "I have to go to work," I say and hop off the couch.

18

*Jonah tried to dis God by refusing to go to Nineveh as God
commanded. The poor guy was thrown into the sea and sat
in a fish's belly for three days as punishment (Jonah 2:1).
Didn't Jonah know you can't hide from God—He knows
everything. My boyfriend, however, doesn't. (Except when my
friends open their big mouths.)*

Avi insists on accompanying me to work.

When we enter the elevator again, I want to tell him
everything that's been on my mind and why I'm confused.
But there's no time. My life is spinning out of control and
there's no button or switch to stop it. Time sucks that way.

"Avi," I say. I don't really have anything to tell him, I
just want him to stop looking away from me.

"Yeah?" he says, turning to me. I wish I could tell what
he's thinking.

"I'll see if I can get some time off work this week so we
can do some Chicago sightseeing."

"I don't need sightseeing, Amy."

He doesn't have to say he came here for me. The fact

that he came all this way to spend a week in Chicago is flattering and overwhelming at the same time.

At the Perk Me Up! counter, I introduce Marla to Avi. Marla smiles wide and drops the cup she's holding so she can shake his hand. Then she giggles, which I've never seen her do before.

When I first met Avi it was a really confusing and awkward time in my life. To be honest, I was rebelling. Avi is the only guy who has ever challenged me. He stayed in the fight long enough to duke it out…mentally, of course. He's as strong on the inside as he is on the outside.

I'm taking care of customers. Avi sits on one of the big cushy chairs and waits. He's leaning back with his arms crossed in front of his chest and I can't believe he's actually here while I'm making skim vanilla lattes instead of spending time with him.

I glance over at him every time I have a free second. And when there's nobody else in the café, I ask Marla if I can make Avi one of my fave hot chocolate drinks.

"You didn't tell me he was visiting," Marla whispers while I'm mixing the drink.

"Yeah, well I didn't know. My dad did, though," I inform her as I top off the cocoa with a triple dose of vanilla-flavored whipped cream.

"And he forgot to tell you?"

"I guess they wanted it to be a surprise." I have yet to tell my dad I hate surprises. Surprises are like having your period in the middle of class. Initially you're shocked and confused, then you're embarrassed and have to deal with everyone staring at you. I'm self-conscious enough as it is; I don't need surprises in my life to make me feel more aware of people gawking at me.

Marla holds out a cup holder for me so I can slip it onto the perfectly made hot cocoa. "I miss my teenage years," she says with a wistful smile on her face. "Boys, school, friends. Enjoy it before you grow up and have more responsibilities than you ever signed up for."

I already feel like I have more responsibilities than I signed up for. And I'm only seventeen.

My specialty drink in hand, I walk over to Avi just as the door to Perk Me Up! opens. It's Jessica.

"I heard about what happened at the dog park today. Amy, are you okay?" Her hair is brown and stick-straight and her eyes look darker than usual because she's wearing a black top. It takes her a second to focus on the guy in the chair, but when she does, a little shriek escapes from her mouth. "Avi?" she asks, totally pointing like a little kid.

Avi stands and I clear my throat. "Jessica, this is Avi. Avi, this is my best friend Jessica."

"Call me Jess," she says, smiling so wide I think her cheeks are going to crack and her lips stretch out so much she reminds me of that elastic woman from the cartoon movie.

"Why didn't you tell me he was coming?" she says through gritted teeth although Avi can hear every word that's coming out of her mouth. Duh! He's standing right here.

"I didn't know," I say back. "It was a surprise."

"Oh."

Jess knows I hate surprises, thus the understanding "Oh" comment.

"What happened at the dog park today?" Avi asks.

I didn't really want to share the disaster so I just say, "Um…"

"Mutt humped another dog and impregnated her right in front of everyone," Jess blurts out. "The owner of the other dog almost called the cops."

"It was no big deal," I say, trying to blow it off. Well, at least I'm trying to make it look like I'm blowing it off. It actually is a major deal and my dad is going to kill me when he finds out Princess's womb is ruined because of my dog. And the fact that he might be a grandpa to a basketful of puppies in a few months.

"Amy, are you *kidding*? *Everyone* knows," Jess says.

Avi leans forward with a confused look on his face. "Why didn't you tell me?"

"I…I don't know." It's the truth.

I'd like to give Avi the hot chocolate concoction I made him, but the whipped cream is melting and running down the side of the cup onto my hand and it doesn't look as decadent and appetizing as it did before Jess came in the café. And now my hand is all grody and sticky from the melting, now lopsided whipped cream.

"I'm going for a walk," Avi says, obviously upset I've shut him out. I can't even blame him for being pissed as I watch him open the door and step out into the cold. I wish I could tell him what's going on, but how can I express it to him when I don't even have it all figured out.

So now it's just Jessica and me standing together. "Ooh, can I have that?" she says, eyeing the drink in my hand.

I shove my "Avi peace offering" at her and go back to working behind the counter.

Why can't things go my way? Is this God's way of entertaining me so I don't have a boring life? I swear, for once I'd like to have a calm, uneventful day.

Marla is in the middle of blending the new Tango Mango Crème Blend for a customer. The entire café now smells like mangoes.

"Can I have the rest of the week off?" I ask her. "I'll work double the hours next week."

"It's okay with me."

Jessica has parked herself at a computer terminal when I start wiping down the tables. "Can you please *not* tell Avi about my life?" I ask her.

"Why not?"

"Because if I want him to know something, I'll tell him. He doesn't need to hear it secondhand from my friends."

Jess cocks her head to the side and says, "What are you trying to hide from him, Amy?"

"Nothing."

Okay, that's not the honest truth. I'd like to hide the bad parts of me, and only share the awesome parts. You can't blame me. He's only here for a week. If he knows I screw up all the time there's no way he'll want to be my…non-boyfriend.

I'm seriously sick of referring to him as the "non."

Something in my life seriously needs to change.

19

Even though the Israeli army is strong, I worry about Israel. I pray for the safety of my family living in Israel and my boyfriend who is in the military there. Is there anything I can do to make this a more peaceful world?

I'm almost done with my shift at Perk Me Up! when, you guessed it, Nathan comes sauntering in. He walks up to the counter and says, "Medium green tea with ice, no sweetener."

He doesn't even look at me. He's focused on the sugar packets next to the register. And he's obviously not interested in sugar packets because he doesn't like his drinks sweetened.

Marla is standing next to me, humming a little tune as she's purposely trying not to pay attention to the interaction between me and Nathan.

When I hand Nathan his drink, he says, "Where's Abi?"

"His name is Avi, and you know it."

Nathan takes a sip of his cold tea while looking at me above the rim of the cup. When he stops drinking he says, "Whatever..." mimicking our previous conversation. "Did he ditch you already?"

It wouldn't hurt so bad if it wasn't so close to the truth. "No. Can't you see I'm working?"

"I'm a customer. I think you're supposed to be nice to customers."

I turn to Marla, who is not pretending to ignore our conversation anymore. "Go on," she says. "Don't mind me. This is extremely entertaining. I think I might even start charging admission...or start a Perk Me Up! open mic night."

Taking a deep breath, I shake my head and turn back to Nathan. He's still standing at the counter. The guy won't leave.

He leans forward and whispers, "You don't like me because I'm a geek...dork...lame...weak sauce...whatever you want to label me."

"That's not true," I say.

"Oh, yeah? Then why are you so hung up on this Avi dude? Tell me his brain is as big as his biceps."

"Not that it's any of your business, but as a matter of fact he's really smart. You don't always have to judge people by their grades. Being fun and outgoing and street-smart is important, too."

"If you're so hung up on the guy, why did you kiss me in the elevator? Oh, that's right. You did it as a joke."

"Did not."

"Yeah, right. Plastic girls like you like to play with people's lives. You never think about the consequences of your actions or who you'll hurt."

My mouth goes wide. Is Nathan kidding? I wouldn't kiss him as a joke, or even a dare. I kissed him because I wanted the upper hand. If he started liking me because of our kiss, I could control our relationship. I could make him hate me or like me. I admit it was manipulative.

Nathan's glasses slip on his nose and he pushes them back up. "I bet if I acted cool and dressed cool you'd dump that Avi guy and want to date me."

"Wanna bet?"

The door to the café opens. It's Avi. And he doesn't look happy that I'm talking to Nathan. Nathan must sense my hesitation because he takes his iced tea without sweetener and stomps off to his usual chair to study.

Marla taps me on the shoulder. "You can go, Amy. Your shift is up."

Thank the Lord.

I peel off the yellow apron. I lift myself on my tiptoes and give Avi a huge smooch while wrapping my arms around him. That'll show him how much I missed him, Nathan how much Avi means to me, and everyone else (including Jessica) how important Avi is in my life.

Taking my cue, Avi wraps his arms around me. "Let's get out of here," he whispers against my mouth, then takes my hand and we leave the café together as a couple.

I think the ice has broken between us as we step out into the cold night air. My cell phone rings. It's my dad. "Hey, *Aba*," I say into my phone.

"Did you get a big surprise today?"

"Yep. He's standing right beside me." I'll talk to my dad later about the new "no surprise rule" I'm about to set up.

"Let's all meet for dinner. How about Rosebud?"

Rosebud is an unbelievable Italian place on Rush Street right near our building. On a Saturday night it's one of the most crowded restaurants in the city. "Sure."

"I'll be there in a half hour."

"Cool. See you there."

I hang up and hadn't even realized I was leading Avi away from our building and Rosebud. I notice we're not holding hands anymore. We're headed toward the beach even though Lake Michigan is freezing and the wind is blowing hard enough to make my face freeze up, making it hard to talk.

"I thought if I told you I was coming you'd tell me not to," Avi says. We're still walking, both of us looking straight ahead at the lake peeking through the city streets.

I want to grab his hand and hold it as we walk, but he's got both of his fists stuffed inside the front pockets of his jeans. "I thought you forgot about me," I say.

He gives a short laugh. "I didn't have time, Amy. I was in basic training, remember?"

I'm totally aware that other girls walking past us on the Chicago city streets are checking him out. Will it always be like that? Does he exude that charisma and confidence on purpose? "What if you did have time, Avi?" I ask him. "Would you find someone else, some pretty Israeli girl to replace me?"

"Why? So you wouldn't feel guilty starting a relationship with that guy Nathan?"

"I kissed you in front of him, Avi. Like I'd do that if I liked him."

"You did it to make him jealous," he says matter-of-factly.

"Did not. Besides, you don't even want a real relationship. You made that clear last summer. No commitments, no boyfriend/girlfriend stuff. You know what I tell my friends...that you're my *non*-boyfriend. Do you know how that makes me feel? Well, I'll tell you, Mr. Israeli Tough Guy. It makes me feel terrible, like I'm not worth the time or effort or emotion to put into a real relationship."

I swallow, but it's not easy because my throat is starting to close up from emotion. Most of the time I try to keep my emotions deep inside, far from the surface. So this sucks, doubly so because it's Avi, the one person I don't want to get too emotional with because I know it'll just push him away.

He tries to pull me toward him, but I swat his hand away. I don't want his sympathy. I want his love.

What feels the worst is that I don't even think he's capable of giving it. God knows he'd never say it.

"I don't know what you want," he says, totally frustrated now. "Amy, I'm sorry. I thought we had this all worked out."

"Yeah, well, we don't. Why did you come here? Just to screw around with my life?"

"No," he says, pulling me into his chest and this time

doesn't let me resist. Holding me tight, he whispers into my hair, "I finished combat basic training and am assigned to a specialized fighting unit. The IDF is taking a different approach to terrorism; they're going to teach us how to think, act, and be the enemy." He takes a deep breath and says, "I don't know if I'll get authorization to contact you in the summer when you visit."

20

Jacob had twelve sons. Each became one of the twelve tribes of Israel (Numbers 1:4).
I wonder what tribe my decendants are from. I'm sure the Internet doesn't track birth records from that far back.

It takes a few minutes for me to comprehend what Avi just told me. Specialized fighting unit. Being the enemy. I pull back and look into his eyes. "We're supposed to see each other next summer when I come to visit. You promised me."

"I got time off now instead."

"Where are you going to be living in the summer?"

Avi gives me a small smile. "I'll be traveling a lot."

"In the Middle East?" I ask.

"Yes. And Europe."

"I don't like that," I tell him. "Not one bit." Taking a look at my watch, I realize we better head to Rosebud or my dad will be worried. "My dad's meeting us for dinner," I tell Avi, then start walking but I feel like I'm in a trance.

Avi takes his place right next to me. "Did I freak you out?" he asks.

"Yep." Totally freaked me out. All these thoughts are running through my head, especially the ones where men are captured and tortured and mutilated. I mean, it's inhumane what's going on in the world. I seriously like my life right here, as safe as I could be in a big city like Chicago.

I'm silent the rest of the walk to Rosebud. My dad is already there, sitting and waiting at a table. He waves us over and stands up to shake Avi's hand and to pat him on the back. Does my dad know? Does he have any idea Avi is about to risk his life for Israel just like he did at Avi's age?

I roll my eyes as they immediately start speaking in Hebrew, strange words and sounds pouring out of their mouths super fast. My phone vibrates with a text message. I read it under the table.

> *Jess: Where did you run off to?*
> *Me: Dinner*
> *Jess: Avi ok?*
> *Me: Yep.*
> *Jess: Does he know you XOXOed Nathan?*
> *Me: NO!!!!!!!!!!!!!!!*

The waitress is standing over to our table, but the guys are oblivious.

"I'll have a Coke," I tell her. "No ice. No lemon." There's nothing worse than watered-down Coke.

"Got it. And for the gentlemen?"

The *gentlemen* are gurgling and gargling their way

through a very intense conversation. They're probably talking about Avi's army training because my dad is totally concentrated and impressed with whatever Avi's talking about. Boys and their gun talk…

I just want to forget about guns and army and elite forces these next seven days. I'm going to treat his military service as if it doesn't exist. Ignorance keeps me sane sometimes. "When you're ready to speak English, just wake me up," I say, then lay my head down on the table.

"Sorry, sweetheart," my dad says. "I was just telling Avi your mom is pregnant."

"Thanks, *Aba*," I tell him sarcastically. "I'm sure I couldn't have told him that myself." I don't understand why everyone in my life just can't keep their mouths shut.

As my temperature is rising and my heart is pounding, I feel Avi's hand reach under the table for mine. As soon as our fingers touch, I take a calming breath. It's as if Avi knew I was starting to panic about everything. He gets big brownie points for this.

Even though I'm usually carb-conscious, I can't resist the warm bread at Rosebud. The loaf is crunchy on the outside and soft and warm on the inside. Taking the jug of olive oil, I pour some of the golden liquid onto my little appetizer plate and spoon parmesan cheese on top.

Avi is staring at me strangely. "What are you doing?"

"Tell me you've never dipped bread in oil and parmesan."

"I've dipped pita into hummus," he says.

"Not the same." I rip off a piece of bread and hand it to Avi. "Here, try it."

He tries it and nods. "That's awesome. Totally unhealthy, but awesome."

When our dishes come, Avi digs in to his food with gusto.

His mouth is going to get spoiled eating Chicago food. We have the best restaurants in the entire country, the largest portions, and probably one of the highest obesity rates.

"Are you watching me eat?" Avi asks, slowing his chewing rate.

"I just want to make sure you like it."

"Amy, in the army you get eggs, jam, bread, and slow-cooked meat. As long as I'm not eating any of those, I'm in heaven."

My dad laughs, then goes into a long, detailed story on the horrible food they served when he was in the army. I stop listening when he talks about bees being stuck in the jam. The rest of the dinner is okay, except that it's mostly my dad and Avi talking and me just wondering when I can get some alone time with my non-boyfriend.

I guess now is better than ever to break it to my dad before he finds out from someone else. "Mutt kind of had an incident this afternoon at the dog park."

Both of them look at me.

"What kind of incident?" my dad asks.

I start peeling away the nail polish from the manicure I just had. "He sort of impregnated Princess. Well, I'm not one hundred percent sure, but Mr. Obermeyer seems to think he did and he's more of an expert on these things than I am."

My dad's hand slaps over his face and he squeezes his eyes shut. "Please tell me you're joking."

"Mr. Obermeyer almost called the police." Then I blurt out, "But he didn't, so it's okay."

"Okay? *Okay?* Amy, I told you Mutt needs to be fixed."

I throw my hands up in the air and say, "I get it, Dad."

"A little late, don't you think?"

I stand up, glad the meal is over, and start walking out of the restaurant. The last thing I need is for Avi to see me and my dad fight. He probably already thinks I'm the drama queen everyone accuses me of being.

Avi catches up to me at the front door. "Amy," he calls out.

I stop and turn around. "I'm not the girl you thought I was, Avi. I screw up my life, like ninety-nine percent of the time. I'm like a mistake that won't stop." I was born a mistake and will always be one.

Avi grabs my shoulders and makes me face him. "Say one good thing."

"Huh?"

"One thing that's not a mistake. One thing you don't screw up."

I search through the recesses of my brain to come up with something, with no luck. "That's the problem, Avi. I screw up *everything*."

My dad comes out of the restaurant before we can finish our conversation. He looks tired and worn out.

"*Aba*, I'm sorry about the Mutt fiasco," I say. "I didn't mean for it to happen."

"I know," my dad says. "I know," he repeats. "Listen, I'll take care of Mr. Obermeyer, Amy. You just keep a better eye on Mutt. Deal?"

"Deal."

We start walking back to the condo and Avi takes my hand in his, then blows on my fingers with his warm breath. It feels so good. I want to moan and give him my other hand, too, but then I'd have to shuffle sideways and that would be dorky.

At the condo, Mutt runs into the foyer so fast he can't stop on the tile floor and flies into the wall. I look over at Avi, who's smiling with those sexy lips of his that were on mine a few hours ago. Avi, his lips, and that kiss stressed me out.

Right now, those lips formed in a tender smile make me less stressed.

"Mutt needs a walk," I say, then grab his leash and clip it to his collar.

I have to say, that's one negative thing about living in the city. In the 'burbs, people just open their doors and dogs run outside in their own yards and do their thing. In the city, it's a whole ordeal. Poop bags, leashes, elevators…

"I'll take him," my dad says, stepping forward and taking the leash from me.

"Cool." I give him a kiss on the cheek. "Thanks, *Aba*."

My dad says something in Hebrew to Avi which I obviously can't understand. Avi steps away from me. Oh, God, I hope my dad didn't warn Avi away from me like he did over the summer. Sometimes fathers can be too overprotective. If anything, this summer Avi was the one who stopped us from going too far physically, not me. It was like one minute I was a sane sixteen-year-old who had always vowed to be a virgin when I got married to one who was questioning everything because I was caught up in the moment with a guy who I had a major connection with.

"Be good," my dad says right before he leaves us alone in the foyer.

Parents shouldn't say "be good." If they know teenagers rebel against authority, saying "be good" to a teen is asking for trouble. I'm tempted not to "be good" just to show him how independent I am.

"What are you thinking?" Avi asks.

I swallow, hard. "Nothing. Nothing at all."

"You seem nervous. You don't have to be nervous."

Yeah, I do, when I'm thinking about being a rebel. "I'm not," I say, then start walking backward. "Do you want a tour of the condo?"

"*Ken.*" I know enough Hebrew to know that *ken* means "yes."

I start rambling while showing him the kitchen, the bathroom, the office, my dad's room, and finally my own bedroom.

In my room, Avi eyes the perfumes on my dresser and the messy, unmade bed. I lean down nonchalantly and pick up yesterday's panties off the floor and throw them into the closet with the rest of the clothes I have to wash. "I'm not usually this messy, and if I knew you were coming and you didn't *surprise* me, I would have actually cleaned up for you."

Avi picks up a picture of me, Jessica, and Cami on Halloween last year. We dressed as the three blind mice. We all wore black leotards with tails, ears, and black sunglasses. "Cute," he says.

I sit on my bed and hug an old Care Bear my mom bought me when I was six and had gotten my tooth knocked out when I was learning how to ride a bike. She let go and instead of me pedaling faster, I turned my head to make sure she was still holding on. When I realized she wasn't, I totally panicked and stopped so fast the bike fell over and I hit the pavement teeth first. I was okay, until I saw my mom's face. She was panicked, and when I wiped my mouth with the sleeve of my shirt and saw it full of blood, I cried so hard it took me over an hour to stop doing that heavy, jerky I'm-trying-to-stop-crying-but-can't breathing.

I bet if Avi saw me back then, in hysterics and snot running down my bloody face, he wouldn't think I was so cute.

I've grown up since then. Well, sort of. I still hate riding bikes. I prefer walking. And deep water scares me, but Avi already knows that.

Avi studies my tennis trophies I won, lined up on my shelf. "You still play?" he asks.

"Not on the team." I didn't make the team this year, partly due to the fact that I didn't go to tennis camp last summer. It's also partly because I've been really busy with conversion class and hanging with friends. Being on a team at CA is totally time-consuming and I missed a whole day of tryouts to go on Jess's parents' boat the day before they were going to sail it to Wisconsin and dock it there for the winter. Before this year I would have never thought anything was more important than getting on the tennis team.

Avi focuses on the picture of him on my nightstand. "I remember that picture. It was your last day in Israel."

"It was before you were in the army."

He nods slowly.

"Do you hate it?"

"What, the army? I'm proud to serve my country, if that's what you mean. All guys get a high on the range, shooting a weapon so strong it could take out an entire three-story building. Makes you feel invincible."

"But you're not."

"You learn that, too. Especially during combat training. With an instructor trained in kicking ass, watch out."

"Eww." I'd be flunking combat training for sure. I'm not into physical pain, inflicting it on myself OR others. It's no surprise Mutt isn't neutered.

"It's not the torture that'll mess with people. It's the mind games." Leaning back on my dresser, he catches his bottom lip with his teeth and looks straight at me.

He looks so adorable I just want to run over to him and hug him tight until I feel all safe and secure in his arms. "What?" I say, totally self-conscious that he's staring at me as if he's memorizing my face.

"I think of you. During the toughest training, when my mind gets weak and I have dark thoughts, I've thought of you."

"Me? I'm Disaster Girl, remember?"

"No. You're the only girl I know who expects life to be perfect and gets pissed off when it's not. You're the girl who's not only beautiful and has a kick-ass body, but you're funny when you don't mean to be and would rather eat dirt than back down from a fight."

"I hate most things."

"Give me one thing you hate."

"Olives."

"But you love sushi."

"I'm not fond of my stepdad, Marc."

"But you're close with your dad now."

"My room is messy."

His eyes rest on my closet and the clothes bursting out of it. "Yeah, it is."

Taking my Care Bear, I throw it at him. He catches the stuffed animal with one hand. "Be careful who you throw things at, Amy."

"Why? What're you going to do?" I take one of my pillows and fling it at him. With his free hand, he catches it without flinching.

He cocks an eyebrow. "You're just asking for trouble."

"I'm already trouble." Picking up my last pillow, I pull it back. "You have no more hands," I tell him. "What are you going to do now?"

Before I have a chance to fling it, Avi pounces on the

bed and pins me down while holding my hands at my sides and my legs with his feet.

"Is this what you learned in combat training?" I ask him, laughing and trying to escape so I can best him, but no such luck. The guy is pure, lean muscle. I'll bet he has, like, zero percent body fat. I'll bet my boobs alone have more body fat than his entire body.

He's sitting on top of me, but with just enough weight for it not to hurt. "Judge your enemy's strengths…and weaknesses," he says.

"Am I the enemy, Avi?"

"Are you? Because right now I can sense you're scheming. That overactive mind of yours is planning an escape."

"How did you know?"

"I can see it in your eyes," he says. "And I feel the adrenaline radiating off your body."

My heart is beating fast and I'm anxious, but not because I want to escape. I haven't been this close to a boy since this summer, when Avi and I went touring through Israel. I want him to kiss me now, like before. But he doesn't. Why?

"Amy, I'm back!" I hear my dad's voice yell from the foyer. Avi jumps off my bed faster than he got on it and reclaims his position leaning on my dresser.

When my dad peeks his head in the doorway of my room, he looks from me to Avi. I've managed to sit upright, but my comforter is all messed up and I'm sure my hair isn't much better.

"Avi, why don't you wait in the living room while I talk to Amy a minute."

Avi rubs his hand over his crew cut, stalling, and I can tell he wants to stay and be my protector.

"Dad, you're embarrassing me," I say after I tell Avi to wait in the living room so he doesn't have to hear my dad's lecture.

"This won't take long, Amy. Just cool it."

"If it's about sex, Mom already told me about it."

"Yeah, well now you're going to get the Dad version, okay?" He rubs his hands together as if he's about to do some heavy weightlifting. The noise of his dry hands making sandpaper sounds makes me wish I'd forced him to buy the hand cream the manicure lady suggested he get. He clears his throat and says, "No sex."

"Got it. Thanks for the talk, Dad. Totally helped. Glad we're on the same page."

"Amy…" he says in a warning tone.

I moan, situate my pillows which are strewn across my bed, and lean back on them. "What?"

"Avi is eighteen, a man. You *just* turned seventeen—"

"Over a month ago," I interrupt.

"Yes, well, guys are different than girls. Guys, um, have urges and, um, so you have to be careful, and uh, your own body is changing and, uh, you know. You might be having, um, feelings, too…"

All those ums and uhs are making my brain twitch.

"*Aba*, maybe you should have gone to that seminar our school had last year about talking to your kids about sex.

Mom went. She said to be careful; there's a lot of diseases. And to protect myself at all times, no matter what. And that if a guy tells me I have to do something in order for him to like me, then I should give him the old heave-ho. And that the risks of having sex at my age *so* outweigh the benefits. And that I can still be a teenager and liked without exploiting myself or my values. Does that cover it?"

He looks stunned. "I guess so."

"Don't you trust Avi?"

"Honey, I don't trust any guy with my daughter. And something funky was going on here between you two before I came back."

"*Aba*, nothing was going on."

My dad bends down, picks up my Care Bear from the floor, and tosses it to me. "You can't pull the wool over these Israeli eyes."

"You're an Israeli with paranoid eyes," I tell him.

"That's a good thing. Call it an occupational hazard. We need to set up a few rules now that Avi's here."

I hate the word "rules." It diminishes your fun, freedom, and spontaneity. "Hit me with 'em," I say, knowing it's no use arguing.

"No boys in your bedroom. You and Avi can hang out in the family room, living room, and kitchen."

"*Aba*, I was just giving him a tour of the condo."

"Sure," he says, obviously not believing me. "Rule number two: no sneaking out to the living room to visit Avi in the middle of the night."

"Why don't you just lock me in the room so I don't escape," I say sarcastically.

"Don't tempt me, Amy."

I roll my eyes. "Dad, a lot of my friends are more experienced than I am."

"That's their parents' problem, not mine."

I stand and face him. "I mean, if I wanted to do something I'd have done it. I'm not ready. Don't worry."

Before he can continue his lecture, I open the door and find Avi. He's going through his duffle in the living room.

"Everything okay?" he asks.

"I got the sex lecture," I tell him.

"Avi, *boyenna b'vakasha*," my dad calls out.

Oh, no. "What did he say?"

Avi stands. "I think I'm about to get the sex lecture, too." He walks to the back of the condo, where my dad is.

Oh, great.

Why doesn't my dad trust me? I mean, I'm not the kind of kid who usually rebels by hanging out with druggies and drinkers. I'm clean cut. Okay, so I've stolen my dad's credit card and this summer I had feelings for Avi that surprised me…and I tested those feelings. But isn't that what teenagers are supposed to do?

I eye Avi's open duffle. Not much in there besides jeans, socks, shirts, and underwear—those tight boxer-ones like the ones in the Calvin Klein ads.

Behind me someone's clearing their throat. I jerk myself up, startled, and turn to Avi.

He nods, then says, "I got the sex lecture."

"Was it harsh?"

"Let's just say your dad tried to convince me he has the knowledge to kill me with one finger."

My dad walks into the room, looking pretty smug I might add. Sure, he just threatened Avi's life if he probably so much as looked at me.

"Arg!"

Mutt is oblivious as he takes a squeaky hamburger in his mouth and drops it at my feet. I pick it up and throw it down the hallway. He bolts after it and brings it back for another round.

"I met with Mr. Obermeyer downstairs when I took Mutt for his walk," my dad informs me as he watches Mutt slide past him. "We had a long talk, which seems to be the theme of my day."

"And?"

"And he said he's taking Princess to the vet tomorrow to see if she's pregnant. If she is, we'll deal with the consequences then."

"Thanks, *Aba*."

"It'll all work out; don't worry. Listen, I've got some work to do and you've got school tomorrow, so I think you should both say your goodnights and go to bed."

Since Avi's bed is the couch, I pull out of the hall closet bed linens and a blanket. I feel Avi's eyes on me as we make the bed together. "I wish we were back in Israel," I say. "This summer we had no rules to deal with, nobody telling us what we can and can't do…it was awesome."

"This is your dad's territory, his house, and his rules."

"Goodie for me." Isn't this my territory and my house, too? When can I start making my own rules up? Or be trusted enough not to have any rules?

When the couch is transformed into a bed, I turn to Avi. "You can use the bathroom to get ready first."

"*Todah*," he says, grabbing a toothbrush, toothpaste, and blue flannel pants.

"You're welcome."

I hurry into my room and dress in a tank and shorts, my usual pajama attire. I sit on my bed and stare at the picture of Avi on my nightstand and can't believe he's really here . . . in my house, in my life again. It's not as perfect as it was in Israel, but there's something about Avi that calms my soul.

At the same time, I try to warn myself that he's only here for a week and not forever. He's leaving soon and I'll be left alone again...no date for the Valentine's Dance, no date for New Year's Eve, no date for Valentine's Day, and no date for the Fourth of July fireworks if the summer trip to Israel doesn't go through.

Nathan'll be around, though. Every day.

Why am I thinking about Nathan when Avi is here? I don't even like Nathan, or his emerald eyes.

Surely I gave Avi enough time to change and brush his teeth. But the door to the bathroom opens just as I reach it and Avi comes out...shirtless, with his hair wet from showering.

Bronzed skin, chocolate eyes, hair that looks almost black when wet. "Hi," I say.

He rakes his fingers through his wet hair. "Sorry I took so long. I needed a shower. I felt dirty from the flight and all."

"I think I'm gonna need that sex talk again," I whisper, then give him a self-conscious smile and move past him to lock myself in the bathroom.

Looking at myself in the bathroom mirror, I wonder what makes Avi think I'm on the same level looks-wise as him. My teeth aren't perfect, my top lip disappears when I smile, my hair is too frizzy, and my boobs are a cup size too big. I even kept my bra on with my pjs because I don't want Avi noticing how much my *boobage* sags when I unleash "the girls."

He said that he likes me because I expect life to be perfect. Who doesn't fight for things to go their way? I guess some people, even Jessica, settle for the status quo. It's in my nature to fight. I guess I can blame that trait on my dad.

I've also come to realize that with turning seventeen, I've become boy crazy. I think about them all the time. It started when I met Avi, and hasn't stopped. Sometimes I'll think about boys at the strangest times, like in conversion class or even when I'm shopping. Last week when Jessica was telling me about her dance competition, my mind wrapped around the word "dance" and my thoughts wandered to when I was in Israel this past summer at a disco and I watched Avi dance. He's an amazing dancer, so comfortable moving his body to music, unlike most guys I know.

Maybe the rules are a good thing, after all.

I peek into the living room before I go to bed. Avi is

laying on the couch, the blanket covering his bottom half but his toned chest is exposed. He's got one arm resting behind his head, which makes his bicep tense up.

"What?"

"Are you on steroids or something?"

He laughs. "You ever try holding a Kalashnikov assault rifle over your head while walking five kilometers in water up to your waist twice a day. Your arms would be just as big. The gun touches the water, you get another kilometer tacked on."

No thank you very much. "I thought you trained in the desert."

"We did that, too. It's either holding the *jerikon* full of water, which is over twenty kilos, or being one of four supporting the heaviest guy in the unit on a stretcher while running. And no matter where you are, if the unit leader tells you to drop on the ground, you go down...whether it's on sharp rocks or not."

"How did you get the scars on your arms?" I ask, now focused on the raw skin on his forearms.

"Ground-crawling exercises. Fun stuff. Now can we stop talking about the army?"

"What do you want to talk about?" I sit on the edge of the mahogany coffee table in front of the couch.

"Tell me about your city. What makes it so special?"

Chicago is unique, unlike any place in the world. I can say just one thing about it and start rambling. "We have world-famous museums, the largest indoor aquarium, every sport team you could imagine with dedicated-to-the-death fans. We have Lincoln Park Zoo, one of the only free zoos in the country and the Harold Washington library, which is the largest of its kind in the world. We have three of the tallest buildings in the world and the best food in the entire country, which includes pizza, sushi, hot dogs, and Italian beef. You want me to go on?"

Avi sits up. "Your eyes light up when you talk about your city."

"I love Chicago. I was born at Weiss Memorial not too far away from here and have lived here my whole life. My mom moved to the suburbs so now I live with my dad. I can't stand not being here. The energy of the city is contagious. My mom and her new husband are having a baby in their new house, anyway, and don't need me hanging around."

"Does it bother you that they're going to have a kid?"

I chip more polish off my nails. "Yeah. It's going to change our whole family. Just when I'm trying to get used to a permanent man in my mom's life, I now have to deal with a baby. It's totally strange. I'm, like, confused about where my family begins and where it ends. No small nuclear family for me. In fact, I don't even know who my immediate family is anymore."

I've never been a fan of change, and my life has changed way too much in the past six months.

"Amy, I thought you were in bed," my dad says from the hallway.

"I was just saying goodnight to Avi."

My dad watches us as if he's a guard in the Israeli military.

"*Lyla tov*, Amy," Avi says, then winks at me.

I guess my night is over, whether I want it to be or not. "Goodnight," I say, then go back to my room and text Jessica.

Me: You there?

Jess: Yep, was waiting 4 u to text me. How's the hottie?

Me: Kewl

Jess: What, no details?

Me: There are none

Jess: Liar. U kiss him yet?

Me: Yes

Jess: And?

Me:

Jess: What's wrong?

Me: Wasn't the same.

Jess: Can I have him, then?

Me: NO!!!!!!!!!!!!!!!!!!!!!!!!!!!!!!

Jess: Just kidding. Gee, Amy, no need 2 yell. Didn't know u were so territorial.

Me: I'm not. OK I am.

Jess: U confuse me.

Me: I confuse myself. And I'm tired.

Jess: Me, 2

Me: I'm going to bed. C u tomorrow.

Jess: Bye, chica

Me: Lyla tov

21

Oil production of Saudi Arabia: 9.475 million barrels per day
Oil production of Iran: 3.979 million barrels per day
Oil production of Iraq: 2.093 million barrels per day
Oil production of Egypt: 700,000 barrels per day
Oil production of Syria: 403,800 barrels per day
Oil production of Israel: 2,740 barrels per day
Do you think Moses made a wrong turn somewhere?

The next day I leave Avi with a map of Chicago and a key to our condo before I catch the bus to school. No amount of begging my dad to stay home and ditch the algebra/trig test today so I can stay home with Avi worked. Nathan isn't at the bus stop, so I'm standing alone. On the bus, Jess is eager to grill me.

"So? How was it last night after we texted each other?" she asks before I even sit down.

"Uneventful. I went to bed." And neglected to do my homework, but I'm hoping to ignore that issue until I'm forced to deal with it. A person can only handle so much at one time.

"And this morning?"

"I took a shower, ate breakfast with Avi and my dad, and left for school."

Jess looks disappointed there isn't more to the story. I am, too. I wish I had more exciting news to tell her, but I'm not about to make anything up.

"I hear you're going to be a mom," Kyle says from the seat behind us.

"Don't know yet," I say, playing along so no one realizes how freaked out I am about Mutt's little escapade yesterday.

Mitch, who has been hiding in the back row of the public CTA bus in an obvious attempt to avoid being confronted by a jilted Jessica, says, "Dude, that dog is an *animal*."

Yes, he is. And yes, he's mine.

"Where's Nathan, Amy?" Roxanne asks.

"How would I know?"

"He's your boyfriend, isn't he? Or are you just going to the Valentine's Dance with him out of pity?"

Pity? Nathan doesn't need pity from me. Okay, so he needs a new wardrobe…but not pity.

"For your information," Jess says, turning around, "Amy has a boyfriend, and he's in town visiting her. Nathan was just a…a brain fart."

Oh, I'm sure Nathan will definitely appreciate being described as a fart. Sometimes Jess gets me in more trouble than I'm already in and has no clue she's done it.

"You guys should come to my place tonight," Kyle says.

"My p's are out of town. A bunch of us are gonna hang out."

Jessica says, "I can't."

"What about you, Amy? You can even pick one of the guys in your harem to bring," Kyle says.

It is Friday, and I am committed to showing Avi a great time while he's here. It wouldn't hurt to stop by Kyle's and hang out. Avi might actually like it. In the dark recesses of my mind, I'm a little excited to show Avi off to Roxanne, who'll inevitably show her face. She's always hanging on Kyle and his friends like one of those disgusting neck skin tags.

I find myself promising I'll be at the party with Avi. I turn back around and lean in to Jessica. "Where are you going tonight?"

"Youth group meeting."

Oops. I forgot I was supposed to go with her and Miranda again. "Are you upset if I don't go with you guys? I mean, Avi is here and all..."

"That's cool," she says. "We're supposed to do a scavenger hunt together, but Miranda and I can do it without you."

I think Avi would think a scavenger hunt with the teen youth group would be lame. I'm convinced he'll have a better time at a party where everyone is dancing and hanging out. Besides, I think he's had enough organized activities in Israel lately; he doesn't need another one while he's on vacation.

During lunch, Jess is sitting at Miranda's table and not at our usual spot. Nathan is sitting next to Miranda. They're all in a deep conversation.

I take my tray of the Chef's Pizza Special and sit next to Jessica. "What's so interesting?"

Miranda glances up and then back down at the paper she was writing on. She mumbles, "We're figuring out strategy for tonight."

"For the youth group thing?"

Jess looks up. "Yeah. We're dividing the city up into monuments, parks, and sports arenas."

I look up at Nathan. "Are you going?"

He puts his arm around Miranda and smiles at her. "Miranda invited me."

The poor girl looks nervous. "You don't mind, do you, Amy?"

"Why would I mind?"

"Well, you guys seem pretty close and everyone thinks you two have something going on." She says it as a statement and a question.

"Nathan has a girlfriend," I inform her.

"And Amy has a boyfriend," Nathan blurts out.

"Wait, I don't get it. If you have a boyfriend and he has a girlfriend, why are you going to the Valentine's Dance together?"

I open my mouth to say something, but nothing comes out.

Nathan takes his arm from Miranda's shoulder. "Now *that* is a great question."

"So what's the answer?" Jess asks impatiently.

"Well, since Avi will be back in Israel, and Bicky...well, I'm not convinced she's real but if she's not a figment of

Nathan's imagination she's, nonetheless, not in Chicago. So we're going together…as friends. Right?"

Nathan puts his hands up. "That pretty much sums it up, except for the part about my girlfriend being a figment of my imagination. She's real."

"What school does she go to?" Miranda asks.

Instead of answering, Nathan gathers his lunch, shoves it into his bag, and stands up. "I just remembered I forgot to study for my chem exam. I'll catch you guys after school."

"Sure thing," Jessica says. "What's his issue?" she asks when he's out of earshot.

Looking at the door Nathan just bolted out of, I say, "No clue. But if you guys find out, you gotta tell me. He lives with his aunt and uncle, he doesn't talk about his past or his parents, and never talks about any brothers or sisters. Something's off."

"Maybe he's an undercover police officer investigating something illegal at school. Or maybe he's a reporter doing an exposé on private schools."

I roll my eyes. "Miranda, I think you've been watching too much television." Nathan is definitely a teenager, as messed up and confused as I am.

I catch up to that messed up kid at his locker after school. "Miranda thinks you're an undercover reporter doing an exposé on private schools…or a cop." With those glasses and skinny frame you'd think he was Clark Kent. Nah, he's too skinny and wouldn't be able to fill out any Superman outfit.

"Cool."

"So, what's your deal? Why are you living out of a suit-case? Why do you bring flowers to someone every week? Why do you say you have a girlfriend but she's never around?"

Nathan shoves his books into his backpack. "Why do you care?"

"I don't know."

He slings the backpack around his back and glares at me. "Well, when you do know maybe then I'll tell you."

22

I was preparing for conversion class today and read the Bible scenario if a man suspects his wife was not a virgin when they got married. The woman, if found guilty, gets stoned to death by the men in her village. If the man is found to be proven wrong, he gets fined and flogged (Deuteronomy 22:18). I seriously need to have a talk with Rabbi Glassman about this. Because there are just so many things wrong with this scenario.

I take Avi to Kyle's party in the evening, ready to show my boyfriend off to all my school friends (besides Jessica, Miranda, and Nathan, who are doing the temple youth group scavenger hunt). With a huge smile on my face, I take Avi's hand and lead him through Kyle's condo. It's bigger than my dad's—Kyle's dad owns one of the best steak houses in Chicago and likes to show off his wealth with big cars, big condos, and big boats.

In the kitchen, Kyle passes out cans of beer. "Dude, you must be Amy's boyfriend," Kyle says with a slurred voice. He's plastered.

Avi declines the beer and Kyle tosses the can to me.

"You're not drinking, are you?" Avi asks.

To be honest, I think beer is gross. "Nope," I say, and toss the can back to Kyle, who mumbles something under his breath about sober people being boring.

Leading Avi to the back of the house where most of the crowd has gathered, we find an unoccupied chair. Avi sits on it and I park myself on his lap.

The music is loud in the back room, almost to the point that my ears are pounding to the bass of the song. While everyone else is either drinking or making out or trying to talk above the music, I lean into Avi's chest while he holds me close.

When I catch sight of Roxanne arriving, I quickly turn my head toward Avi and start to kiss him. Our lips touch first, then I slide my tongue over his while I slip my arms up his chest and around his neck. As I pull back, I lick my lips and give him a sexy, knowing smile.

He nuzzles his mouth close to my ear and says, "Why the big show?"

I turn my head and try to say to him so only he can hear me above the blaring song, "Don't you want to kiss me?"

"Yeah. But not with a bunch of drunk kids watching us."

"Are you saying I'm a kid?"

Before he answers, I hear Roxanne's squeaky voice saying, "Hi, Amy. Hi, Nathan."

I look up. Roxanne is standing next to us, her fingers over her open mouth while she gasps. "Oh, I'm sorry. I thought you were Nathan."

I'm in trouble. Avi is expressionless, but his arm loosens from around my waist.

"Why would she think you were kissing Nathan?" he asks me.

I clear my throat. "I can explain." Roxanne is still standing over us, a wicked smirk painted on her face. "Do you mind?"

Ignoring me, Roxanne holds out her hand. "I'm Roxanne."

"I'm Avi," he tells her in his slow, sexy Israeli accent as he shakes her hand. I swear she turns her hand as if she expects him to kiss the back of it. "I'm Amy's boyfriend from Israel."

Roxanne bursts out laughing. "Oh, I heard about you. So glad you and Amy decided to see other people. You're such an understanding guy."

When he releases her hand, I wave my fingers at her and say, "Shoo, go away." She's like an annoying gnat that I wish I could squash.

Roxanne moves away when Kyle walks in the room with a bottle of champagne.

"Did you kiss Nathan?" Avi asks.

Umm…"No. Roxanne is the enemy, Avi. Don't listen to her. She just likes spreading lies about me."

He stands (I have to pretend not to have fallen off his lap) and walks over to Roxanne. She cocks her head to the side and says, "Wanna play Spin the Bottle? You can, you know, switch partners. Amy likes switching partners, right?"

I try pulling Avi's hand to make him leave the room, but he's planted where he is like a stubborn tree root.

"I don't like people spreading rumors about my girlfriend."

I pull his arm more. "Avi, let's just leave."

Roxanne laughs. "Rumors? Dude, you're the second guy she's been locking lips with this week. And speak of the devil. Hi, Nathan. We were just talking about you and Amy's hot show in the cafeteria."

Oh, man. I'm toast. I look at the door and see Miranda, Jess, and Nathan walking toward us.

The entire room is silent for the moment while the next CD is put into the slot.

"Hey," Jess says. "We finished with the scavenger hunt and wanted to see if you were still here."

Avi knows the truth. He saw the way Nathan and I looked at each other just now. Is the guilt transparent in my eyes?

"You lied to me," he says.

Right in front of everyone he lets go of my hand and leaves me standing here in the middle of Kyle's party.

23

It's not so easy to convert as one might think. I still have to go before three respected Jewish community members called a "Bet Din" and take a verbal test. Rabbi Glassman told me not to stress over it; it's not like the SATs. Life is full of little SAT tests, though, isn't it?

"You made an ass out of me," he says after I catch up with him at the entrance to my building.

"Avi, I'm sorry. I didn't expect you to go up to Roxanne and get details."

He turns to me while we're in the elevator. "You looked me right in the eye and lied to me."

I put my hands up in surrender. "Okay, I admit it. I lied to you. Are you happy now?"

"Don't turn this around to make me the bad guy. Do you always go around kissing guys?" he asks when we reach my floor and step off the elevator. "Where's your loyalty and honor?"

I roll my eyes and say, "We're not in the army now, Avi."

"Maybe we should be."

"What's that supposed to mean?" When I open the door and walk inside my condo I turn to him, "Besides, where's *your* commitment?"

"Please, Amy. What would you know about commitment?"

I open my mouth wide in shock. "Screw you!" I yell, then go to my room and slam the door shut.

I can't remember how long it's been since I had a good cry. You know, one of those cries where you can't catch your breath and just when you think there can't possibly be any more tears coming out of your eyes, a new wave of desperation washes over you and you bawl all over again.

That's the way I'm crying right now. I feel so horrible I messed up with Avi. I feel so horrible that I want to figure out Nathan and what makes him the way he is. Nathan told me I liked Avi because of his looks and warned me if he looked as good I'd be after him, too.

I'm a terrible person. It's not Avi's fault, either. It's mine.

Avi knocks on my door after about a while.

"What?"

"Open the door and let me in."

"You aren't allowed in my room, remember?"

He knocks again, louder. "Then just open the door."

When I do, I see that he's got his duffle slung over his shoulder. "What are you doing?"

"This isn't working. You and I both know it. I'm going to stay with Tarik over at the Northwestern dorms. You remember Tarik, don't you?"

"Yeah, but—"

"He'll be here soon. Listen, Amy…you want to kiss other guys, that's cool. This thing between us wasn't going to last anyway."

"You *told* me not to wait. You *wanted* to be the non-boyfriend, remember?"

"What's in here," he says, pointing to his head, "and what's in here," he says, fist pounding on his heart, "are two different things."

I step forward and hold out my hand, wanting to ease his insecurity and the tension between us. "Avi…come here."

Instead of stepping forward, he steps back and points to his head. "Gotta keep my mind clear," he says. "Remember what I told you about the mind games?"

"Yeah. They're worse than the torture."

"God, I can't tell you how many irrational things are running through my head right now. Kissing you until you can't think straight. Kicking that Nathan guy's ass. Smashing the wall with my fist because you've been looking at other guys."

"I told you I'm the Disaster Girl."

"No, Amy. You've got your life here. Mine is in Israel or wherever the army sends me. It's the way it is; it's the way it was always meant to be. Who were we kidding, thinking this thing between us could work?"

I did, but I don't tell him. He's obviously given up the fight. "You're really leaving?"

"Tarik is probably downstairs waiting for me."

New tears start to come, damn it. I will them to stop, but

they won't. "I don't want you to go." I want to beg, plead, grab his leg and hang on until he agrees to stay...but I can't.

When he pets Mutt and walks to the door, I let him. And then I stay with him and walk outside where I recognize his friend Tarik in a car outside my building. Tarik steps out of the car and gives me a small hug. "Hey, Amy," he says. "It's been a while, huh?"

I wipe my nose and watery eyes with my sleeve. "How's school?" I ask.

"Tough, but I'm getting used to it." Tarik looks from me (obviously overwrought and devastated) to stone-faced Avi. "Um...you want me to get involved in this?"

"No," Avi says emphatically, while I tilt my head to the side and contemplate asking for intervention. Maybe what Avi and I need is third-party arbitration. I learned about arbitration in my social studies class last week and the magic of an unbiased party deciding your fate.

"Well, then...I guess I'll leave you two to say your goodbyes." Tarik heads back to the driver's side, but calls over his shoulder, "If you need me, just give a holler."

I'm tempted to holler.

Avi tosses his duffle into the back seat of Tarik's car, then turns to me. "I'll call you before I leave Chicago."

"I wanted to take you to the top of the Sears Tower. Every tourist has to go there."

"I'll go on my own."

"And what about Oz Park? Did you know the guy who wrote *The Wizard of Oz* lived here?"

"I'll figure it out."

"But what if you don't, Avi? What if you go back to Israel without seeing what Chicago has to offer?"

Avi cups my cheek with his palm. "It doesn't all have to be perfect. Life isn't perfect."

"I want it to be."

His thumb slowly caresses my face. "I know. It's what makes you unique." He squeezes his eyes shut, then says, "I gotta go before I do something stupid."

I watch as he sits in the passenger seat, says something to Tarik, and the car drives off.

After he leaves me alone, crying, and devastated, I want to kneel right here and start bawling all over again.

"You're not crying over that guy, are you?" I hear Nathan's voice behind me.

I face him and squint my eyes accusingly. "Have you been spying on me this whole time?"

"Nope. Why, was it a good breakup? 'Cause if it was, I'm sorry I missed it."

I walk up to Nathan, take my finger, and poke it into his chest. "You are the *rudest*, most *self-centered*, *dragon-eyed*, *inconsiderate*, *egotistical*…" I'm racking my brain to think of more words when Nathan takes my finger into his hand and stops me from poking him again.

Nathan's touch doesn't affect me like Avi's does. And for the first time it's clear Nathan isn't "The One" and never has been. I have a connection to him, but it's oh, so different than the connection I have with Avi.

I'm too weak to do anything else but slump my shoulders and cry. The pain is too great, like someone is ripping open my heart and squeezing it tight. My knees start to buckle and Nathan catches me.

"You really *are* upset, aren't you?" he says, staring at me with his eyebrows down and furrowed in sympathy. I've never seen Nathan have sympathy for anyone, especially me.

I squeeze my eyes shut. "I'm not as plastic as you accuse me of being."

"I guess not. Listen, Amy. I'm sorry. You're right about me. Well, except for the dragon-eyed part."

"What?"

"I played you. I played your boyfriend. It wasn't fair, I know. Sometimes I want everyone's life to be as screwed up as mine. Call it a self-defense mechanism."

He helps me stand. I wipe my nose and eyes with the sleeve of my shirt. "What's so wrong with your life, Nathan? Who are you? Make me feel better about my crappy life by sharing yours."

I understand why I'm insecure: my dad just came back into my life, my mom and her new husband are planning a family without me...and I don't know where my family life begins and where it ends.

"I'm a foster kid. Parents gave me up when I was ten because they couldn't afford all eight kids they had. I've been tossed from one foster home to another since then."

Wait, I don't get it. "I thought Mr. and Mrs. Keener were your aunt and uncle?"

"No other foster home would take me after they took a look at my file, so they were kind of forced into it by the courts. My aunt and uncle aren't on speaking terms with my parents. They cut all ties a long time ago. Something about marrying trailer trash makes you trailer trash."

I can't imagine my parents giving me away. Even when my dad and I weren't talking, he still tried. It was me who pushed him away. My mom raised me since she was in college, going to school and working while trying to juggle having a kid and getting a career going. I admire her so much. I don't think she ever considered giving me up.

"Why do you dress like—"

"Like I'm a dork?"

"Well, yeah."

"My aunt wants me to dress conservative. Thinks if I dress like a bad kid, I'll be a bad kid."

"Are you bad, Nathan?"

He focuses on the ground and shrugs. "I have been. You don't get kicked out of thirteen foster homes in seven years for being a model kid. "

"And now?"

"I guess I'm still fucked up." He looks at me. "I shouldn't have kissed you in front of everyone in the cafeteria. And…I have to admit…I knew your boyfriend was going to be at the party tonight and was secretly happy he found out we kissed. I know I hurt you, Amy."

The truth is I hurt myself. I let my insecurity and confused emotions overcome what I knew deep in my heart was right all along. I play a tough game, but inside I'm weak. Just like Nathan.

I hook my arm through Nathan's and say, "Do you have any ice cream at your place?"

"I think so. Vanilla, maybe."

"That'll do."

"You want to hang out with me?" he asks, totally shocked.

"Yeah. Isn't that what friends are supposed to do?"

"I've got to admit, I haven't had a friend in a long time. Don't know if I even know how to be one."

"What about Bicky?" I ask when we get in the elevator and head to the fortieth floor.

"She's a foster kid, too. I met her in a home in Freeport last summer."

"Where is she now?"

He takes a deep breath and says, "Rehab. She got into some bad stuff and is all messed up. I bring her flowers every Saturday, but they won't let me see her or talk to her. She receives my letters and notes, though."

Wow. And I thought my family life and love life were rough. I have the urge to go hug my mom and dad and thank them for hanging in there with me.

When we step into Nathan's condo, he turns to me. "Will you please change your shirt, it's got snot all over the sleeve. As your friend, I just want to be honest with you."

I look down at my snot-encrusted shirt. It is grotesque. "I'll be right back," I say, then trot over to my door.

I change my shirt and go back to the Keeners' place. When we're in Nathan's room, we hang out on his bed and dig into a tub of ice cream.

I look at Nathan. If you look past his geeky attire, you can see that he could possibly be cool. With a LOT of help.

"What are you looking at?" he asks, turning to me with his bright green eyes.

"I was just thinking that you don't have to dress different to appease your aunt and uncle. You should be yourself. If they kick you out for being you, well...I'm sure you could come live with me and my dad."

"We could be like brother and sister?"

"Yeah," I say, totally serious and meaning every single word. "Like brother and sister. And friends...great friends," I say, taking a spoonful of vanilla ice cream.

Those green eyes are starting to water.

"Nathan, are you crying?"

One lone tear falls down his cheek. "Yeah." He looks down and swipes the tear from his face. "I haven't had a sibling in a long time, Amy."

I hug him. To be honest, I think it's the first sisterly hug he's had in years.

"Do you really play the guitar?" I ask him, eyeing the black leather case on the floor while I try and lighten the mood.

"Used to be in a band, but it's kind of tough being a member of a group when you move as often as I have."

Picking up the guitar, I hand it to him. "Play something for me."

"Like what."

"A song. For me."

"Do you want me to make it up?"

"If you can."

"Okay...let's see. I'll call it 'My Sister Barbie.'"

24

Tzedakah is the commitment a Jew makes to give charity.
Tzedakah doesn't have to be all about money. It can be
doing mitzvahs (good deeds) for others less fortunate, too.
My friend Nathan needs a little Tzedakah thrown his way.

I bring Nathan to my mom's house in Deerfield the next morning for moral support. Last night Nathan convinced me to be honest with her and Marc about questions I have concerning the new baby.

My mom rushes out of the house and hugs Nathan. I think her emotional hormones are in overdrive. "Avi, it's so nice to finally meet you," she says with a big smile. "Amy's told me so much about you."

"Mom—"

"How are you liking being in our big city?" she says, ignoring me. "Amy must be showing you a grand old time."

"Mom, this isn't Avi."

"It's not?"

"No. It's Nathan. Nathan, this is my mom," I say as I unleash Mutt and let him loose in my mom and Marc's house.

"Oh. I thought his name was Avi."

"No, his name is Nathan. Avi is another guy."

"Then where's this Avi?"

"I don't know."

"Oh. Well, Nathan, why don't you come in and have lunch with us."

While we're eating lunch in the kitchen, Nathan kicks me under the table. It's my cue to start bringing up issues I've been avoiding. "When the baby is born, where's it going to sleep?"

My mom looks to Marc. "In our room, at first."

"Well, we only have two bedrooms because the third is used as an office," Marc chimes in.

"What are you asking?"

"Well, I don't want to be sleeping on the couch when I stay here. I want to keep my room. I may not live here permanently, but I still want a room when I visit. It's important to me."

"Can't you share one with the baby?"

I raise my eyebrows and chuckle. "I'm a teenager. Like I really want to share a room with someone in diapers."

Marc puts his fork down while he thinks. "Maybe I can move the office into the basement."

"There's no windows down there and little ventilation, Marc," Mom coos. "What about your allergies?"

"Amy has a point about the room situation. I can take

my allergy medicine before I go down there. Is that fair? You keep your bedroom and the baby will get the office."

I guess Marc isn't such a bad guy, after all. He just needs to get used to having a daughter like me around...and a dog like Mutt. Maybe I should suggest he take his allergy medicine every day.

My mom sits up straight, or as straight as she can with a protruding belly. "As long as we're making concessions, how about if I request one of my own?" she says.

I brace myself. "Shoot."

"After the baby's born, you babysit one weekend night a month. Changing diapers and all."

"Fine. But if it pukes all over my clothes you're paying for the dry cleaning."

"It's a deal."

After lunch, the four of us sit and play Scrabble.

"So...are you two an item?" my mom asks before one of her turns.

"We're just friends," Nathan blurts out.

"Yeah," I confirm. "Just great friends."

Marc wins Scrabble by a landslide with a triple word score with the word zareba. We all challenged him and he won. Zareba is a word, if you can believe it. Then Nathan and I take Mutt for a walk around the block before we head back to the city. It feels good to have Nathan as a friend, to give me the guy perspective on stuff.

My phone buzzes with a text message when we're driving back to the city.

"Can you read it to me?" I ask Nathan.

"It's Jessica. She wants to know why you want Wes's number."

"Text her back and tell her it's a surprise."

I hear Nathan typing away on my cell phone.

"She says you have enough guys in your life and need to take a breather."

I steer the car to the side of the road and grab my cell out of Nathan's hands.

"What are you doing?"

"Bribing my best friend." I smile when she finally texts me Wes's number. I dial it and wait for an answer.

"Wes, this is Amy. You know, the virgin from the youth group meeting."

"I remember. The girl with the dark hair and clear blue eyes. Are you breathing heavy on purpose?"

"No, that's just my dog panting in my ear."

"Yeah, right," he says, totally not believing me.

"Listen, if you ever need a guitar player for Lickity Split, my friend Nath—I mean Nate—Nate Greyson is his name and he rocks."

"I sing, too," Nathan whispers beside me.

"He sings, too," I add.

"We're rehearsing today at Lounge Ax. If he wants to come by and jam with us, that's cool. Can't say he's in the band, but we're always lookin' for subs."

I hang up and toss the phone into Nathan's lap.

"Thanks," he says. "I think I once called you inconsiderate and rude. You're not."

"Yeah, well, you caught me when I'm heartsick and weak."

I tell Nathan to be at Lounge Ax later. I have to pick up Jess and take her to dinner. The bribe dinner.

At Hanabi, our favorite sushi place, I order the Jewish Chef's Special without crab or shellfish, a spicy tuna roll and spicy tuna rice bowls with tempura crunch. Jess orders the Hwe Dup Bob bowl of kosher sushi, lettuce, and brown rice.

Jess takes the first bite of her special concoction and moans with delight. "This is *so* good."

"It better be. It's costing me sixteen dollars."

She shoves another forkful into her mouth. "First Avi, then Nathan…now Wes. I think you've gone off the deep end here. I have to say giving you Wes's cell number was *so* worth this dinner."

Frustrated, I tell Jessica the truth. "The number was for Nathan. He plays guitar and needed guys to jam with."

"So you just spent sixteen dollars on my dinner for doing something nice for Nathan?"

I shove a spicy tuna roll into my mouth and nod.

Jess puts her fork down. "So you're not into Wes?"

I shake my head. "Nope."

"What about Nathan?"

Another shake. "Nope."

"And Avi?"

At the mention of his name, my heart stings. "He's staying at Northwestern with a friend. It's over."

"Why?"

"Because he wants it to be. I kissed another guy, I humiliated him in front of everybody, and because he's in the Israeli military for the next three years."

"Do you still like him?"

"Oh, man, Jess, you can't imagine. It's like he took a piece of me when he left. I really screwed up. I wish I knew where he was, but even if I did I wouldn't know what to say to him."

"Too bad you can't kidnap him."

Yeah. Too bad. If I could kidnap him then I could tell him that it doesn't matter that we're apart. It doesn't matter that I kissed another guy. My heart still belongs to my Israeli soldier and nobody can take that away...not time or a kiss. But why *can't* I kidnap him? Why can't I make him listen to what he might not want to hear? While my mind is churning, I'm getting more excited by the second.

"That's it. Jess, you're a genius!" I say.

She looks at me, confused and clueless. "I think I missed something."

"No, you're right. I need to kidnap Avi. Secret military operation style—it's right up his alley."

"Jess, you don't even know what dorm he's staying in."

"We'll find out. Doesn't Miranda's aunt work in admissions? That's why she thinks she's automatically getting in?"

"Okay, so suppose you know where he's staying. Then what? We're going to handcuff him and take him in a getaway car? I've only seen him a few times, but I know he could overpower the two of us no problem."

She's right. I need more muscle on my side—a guy. "Nathan will help."

"Nathan?"

I convince her he's the only one who'll help. Besides, our kiss was fifty percent his fault.

In the evening, I recruit Nathan and Miranda. Nathan's skeptical, but Miranda's on board. We plan the mission for Friday, after school.

Two days from today.

25

What is God's definition of a family?
I've been trying to figure out my own definition, but I
can't come up with one that makes complete sense.

I'm going to be a grandmother. For real. My dad talked to
Mr. Obermeyer's vet on the phone, confirming the results.
Mutt really is a stud.

Not wanting bad blood with Mutt's father-in-law, I
bake homemade doggie cookies and knock on Mr. Obermeyer's door. The creak on his floor alerts me he's home,
although I'm not sure when he peeps through his peephole
and realizes it's me he'll open the door.

Lucky (or not) for me, he opens the door. He does not
look happy to see me. "What do you want now?"

Holding out the bag of cookies that I tied with a pink
ribbon, I say, "These are for Princess."

His lips unpurse for a millisecond. Opening the door

wider to let me in, I'm not sure I want to actually walk into Mr. Obermeyer's condo. He's probably going to make me take my shoes off to protect his pristine floor and has plastic covering his furniture so nobody gets any marks on it.

I walk inside his place. He's got jazz playing softly in the background. "You like jazz?" I ask, trying to make conversation, at the same time wondering when I can make a smooth exit without insulting the old man. The last thing I want to do is upset Mr. Obermeyer. His grumpy threshold is very thin.

Reaching into the bag, he pulls out a homemade treat and hands it to Princess, who's lying on a pink plushy dog bed with her name embroidered on it. Her water bowl is right next to it. The pampered pooch doesn't even have to get up to drink; she can hang her head over the side of the bed and lap up her refreshment.

What a life!

"Your mutt really messed things up, didn't he?"

I bite my bottom lip. "I know it's my fault, Mr. Obermeyer. And I'll pay for the vet bills and even take all the puppies and sell them after they're weaned if you want so you don't have to look at them more than you have to. Just...I'd appreciate it if you'd not terminate the pregnancy." Tears are coming to my eyes, which sucks because even though I'm emotional I hate to show it to other people.

"Wait here a second," Mr. Obermeyer says, leaving me alone while he disappears down the hall with his feet shuffling slowly across the floor. He shuffles back, holding a picture of an old woman beside a huge silver cup. A poodle is sitting next to her. The woman is grinning from ear to ear. You can tell she's deliriously proud. So is the dog.

"Is that Princess?"

"Yes, with my wife. Esther died last year, right after the dog show." Mr. Obermeyer gazes at the picture longingly. "I miss her."

"I'm sorry I ruined your dog's uterus," I say, taking advantage of the sentimental moment and praying he'll forgive me.

The old man shakes his head. "You didn't ruin her. It's just…well, I'm a little overprotective of Princess."

Ya think? "What about the puppies?"

"My wife wanted to breed Princess and create champion purebreds."

"What do *you* want, Mr. Obermeyer?"

"I just want my wife back."

His dedication to his wife makes me think of Avi. And for the first time since I moved into my dad's building, I can relate to the old man. He's not bitter. He's jealous that I have a dad and friends and he's got nobody. Well, nobody except an ugly dog.

Here I was thinking all along that two people can't possibly make up a family, but I think I was wrong. Yes, it does happen that I'm wrong. Not often, but on the rare occasion.

"Mr. Obermeyer, how about you join us for a family Shabbat dinner next Friday."

"I'm not Jewish."

"You don't have to be Jewish in order to be in my family, Mr. Obermeyer. Just ask my mom."

26

I love the Lord
for He hears my voice, my pleas;
for He turns His ear to me
whenever I call (Psalms 116:1).
Sometimes my brilliant ideas get me in trouble
and I need a little help from above.

"Knit caps?"

Miranda holds out our newly purchased hats for our kidnapping operation. "Check."

"Black clothes?"

Miranda does a scan of me, Nathan, Jess, and herself. "Check."

"Flashlights?"

We all click them on to make sure they're working. "Check."

"Walkie-talkies?"

Jess holds up four Motorola ones her parents use when they go to Disneyland every year so nobody gets separated for too long.

"Handcuffs?"

I hold up the plastic ones I bought at Walgreens.

"Lipstick and scrunchies?"

"Now here's where I draw the line," Nathan says, flicking the light from his flashlight in my face.

"Nathan, obviously I didn't mean you. Miranda, you've got the keys?"

Miranda jingles her keys in front of her. "Got your dad's keys, your dad's car, and the address. You ready for this, Amy?"

Considering my heart is beating a million times a second and I haven't eaten for two days because I've been nervously looking forward to today, I'm ready.

We pile into my dad's Lexus and drive north toward Evanston. Miranda is driving. I'm in the front passenger seat. Jess and Nathan are in back. When we're close, I order everyone to put on their knitted caps from their back pockets.

"Do I have to?" Jess asks. "My hair will get all flat."

I roll my eyes. "Do you think commandos worry about their hair being flat?"

"Amy, we're not real commandos. And Avi will know it's you. This isn't a real military operation. It's a girl who wants her guy back."

It's a real operation to me.

At Allison Hall, we park out front.

"Now what?" Miranda asks.

I scan the area, analyzing the best place to plant ourselves.

"How do you know he's even here?" Jess asks. "He could be out for the night, staying in for the rest of the night…"

"Jess, you're not helping," Nathan chimes in.

Jess shuts up.

"Okay, here's the deal," I say. "Jess, you go inside and ask around. Pretend you're a student and ask if people know where Tarik is."

She puts her hand on the handle to the car door, but pauses before she opens it. "What's his last name?"

"I don't know. But I'm sure there's not an abundance of Tariks in the dorm."

While I watch her saunter to the front doors of the dorm. Manicure be damned, I peel off the remaining nail polish from my fingernails, then start to chew on each nail.

"Stop that," Nathan orders. "Nail biting creeps me out. Listen, if he likes you he likes you and if he doesn't…well, that's his loss. Either way, whether you bite your nails or not isn't going to change the outcome."

"You're heartless," I tell him.

"I'm a realist," he argues.

I disagree. As a person who thinks when life gets shitty you can plow right through the shittiness and change the course of your life, I'm going to do what I can to change it. I do think I can change my destiny.

Every guy who enters the dorm I think is Avi. Every girl who enters the dorm I think is there to see him. Oh, man, I know what Avi means about how dangerous your mind can be.

"Is that him?" Miranda says excitedly for the millionth time.

"No."

Ten minutes go by and my great kidnapping idea maybe isn't so great, after all. When Jessica finally comes back to the car I'm ready to ditch the plan and trek back home.

"Tarik left about a half hour ago with a guy I'm assuming is Avi."

I grill her with questions. "How do you know? Did you ask a guy or a girl? Do they know where they were going? Do you know when they'll be back? Who else was with them?"

"Amy," Jess says. "Why don't you go in there and ask the guy yourself. I got the info you wanted. He's not at the dorm. Do you want to stay and kidnap him when he comes back, or do you want to abort the mission?"

I consider both options. Leaving here means I'm giving up on him…on us. Leaving here means that my insecurities and self-doubt have overpowered and won over my desire to change the course of my life for the better.

"We're staying on course," I tell them.

"Can we abort the stupid knit hats, at least?" Jess asks.

"No."

I hand everyone their walkie-talkies and we sync our channels. "You all know what he looks like, right?"

Miranda bites her bottom lip. "I've only seen him once in real life and once in a picture. It's dark out, but I'll do my best."

"Good enough," I say. "Nathan, you wait by that tree on that side of the dorm and Jess…you wait over there by that statue. When you see Avi, Tarik, or both of them, announce it on the walkie-talkies and we'll surround them. Got it?"

Nathan shoves the black knit cap on his head and heads for the tree with the walkie-talkie in hand.

Jess puts her cap on, but leans over the front seat and turns the rearview mirror toward her so she can see what she looks like. After loosening some curly wisps of tendrils from beneath the cap she says, "I'm doing this because we're best friends, you know."

"I know. And I love you for it."

"Uh huh. You owe me big for this, Amy," she says, and jumps out of the car, marching toward her lookout spot.

"Where are you going to stalk him…I mean, stake him out?" Miranda asks.

I stick the handcuffs in my back pocket and shove my hair under the cap. Then I stumble out of the car, toss my cell phone at Miranda, and say, "I'll be across the street. I've got to have all sides of the building covered."

With a walkie-talkie in hand, the cuffs hidden in my back pocket, and my hair hidden from sight, I seriously feel like I'm undercover.

I sit on a bench at a bus stop across the street from the dorm. And wait. And wait some more. I think we've been on the stakeout for over fifteen minutes.

"Ten-four, do you read?" Jessica's voice calls over the walkie-talkie.

I press the talk button. "Do you see him?"

"No. I just wanted to know what our operation's name is. Every operation has a code name."

"Yeah," Miranda chimes in. "How about Operation Wildcat. You know, for the Northwestern Wildcats."

"How about Operation Kidnap Avi," Jessica chimes in.

"How about Operation Stupidity, *ten-four*," our fourth accomplice chimes in.

"Nathan, shut up," Jessica says.

"I was just wondering…" Nathan says. I'm trying to keep the walkie-talkie on a low sound level so no one else can hear us. I didn't know my recruits were going to be so chatty. "What do you want me to do if I see him?"

Well-thought-out plans are not my strong point. I say, "Stall him."

"How?"

"I don't know…do whatever it takes to stop him," I whisper into my walkie-talkie. "Just make sure he stays still long enough for me to handcuff him and lead him in the getaway car."

"THIS IS NORTHWESTERN CAMPUS SECURITY," an unfamiliar and very authoritative voice comes through the walkie-talkie speaker in my hand. "IDENTIFY YOURSELF AND YOUR LOCATION IMMEDIATELY."

"Don't give out any information," Nathan says. "They'll never find us."

Spoken like a true bad boy.

"I'm scared, Amy," Miranda's voice comes through the walkie-talkie.

I bang my head against the lightpost I'm leaning on. "You just said my name."

"I'm sorry. I didn't mean to. I'm turning this thing off right now."

"THIS IS CHIEF OF SECURITY ON NORTH-WESTERN CAMPUS," the walkie-talkie bellows. "AMY, YOU'RE ON A CAMPUS RADIO FREQUENCY AND WE HAVE YOUR ENTIRE CONFESSION RECORDED. IF ANYONE IS ASSAULTED ON MY CAMPUS, WE'VE GOT EVIDENCE AGAINST YOU."

His threat gets met with silence until Nathan chimes in with, "I'm hungry."

"I'm cold," Jess says.

I think I need new recruits.

Just as I'm about to send everyone home, I see two guys out of the corner of my eye who look just like Avi and Tarik. In fact, I'm sure it's them. I quickly press the talk button. "I see them! Nathan, they're headed to Allison Hall, almost reaching you right now."

I hear a "Stop right now!" and the walkie-talkie goes dead. I run across the street, aware Jessica is behind me trying to catch up.

The area is dark and is surrounded by trees, but I can make out the scene without light. Nathan is moaning on the ground, Avi is in deep commando mode with his hands in fists, and Tarik is standing behind them.

I run and kneel on the ground beside Nathan. "Are you okay? Oh my God, you're bleeding," I screech when the side of his face catches the light.

"He punched me and did that Israeli self-defense stuff on me," Nathan says while staying in the fetal position.

Avi holds his hands up as if he did nothing wrong. "Are you kidding me? You tried to tackle me." He takes a look at me and Nathan, then at Jessica. "Wait, why are you all dressed like burglars?"

"We're kidnappers, not burglars," Jessica corrects him.

"Who're you going to kidnap?"

I stand up and whip out the handcuffs. "You."

Avi looks down at the cuffs dangling from my fingers. "They're plastic."

And cost me a dollar ninety-nine. "Yep. Now turn around and put your hands behind your back so I can complete this mission."

Avi turns to Tarik. "I guess we're not hanging out tonight."

Tarik is smiling wide. "This is better than reality television, man. I'd do what the girl wants."

Following my instructions, Avi places his hands behind his back and I secure the handcuffs to his wrists.

Just as I'm ready to escort him to the car, flashing lights and campus security cars screech beside the sidewalk. Security personnel come running at us from all directions. There's no escape.

"Which one of you is Amy?" a big guy who I swear could double as a WWE wrestler asks.

"Listen," Avi says to the guy, stepping between me and the security guard. "I'm responsible for this whole thing."

"Are you Amy?"

I think Avi is sizing up the guy, seeing if he could take him and his attitude on while handcuffed. My Israeli knight in shining armor.

"I'm Amy," I tell the guy while slowly raising my hand and peeking my head around Avi.

"Amy, I can handle this," Avi says.

"I can, too," I tell him. "Besides, you're handcuffed. I wouldn't be arguing while handcuffed."

Avi gives a short laugh. "Do you ever think there's consequences to your actions?"

"Not usually."

The security guy clears his throat, getting our attention. "Are you done with your private conversation?" Shaking his head, he points at Nathan on the ground, looking like a wounded puppy. "Are you hurt?"

"Yes. And my ego is, too," Nathan responds.

The big guy surveys the situation. "We have a hazing policy on campus," he says. "I warn you; for breaking the policy you not only get stripped of your Greek affiliation, you get kicked out of the university."

"Lucky we're not students here, then," Nathan says groggily.

"Is there a reason this guy is in handcuffs?" the big guy asks, eyeing Avi and getting more annoyed by the second.

Letting out a breath I say, "Okay, here's the truth." I point to Avi. "This is my boyfriend…well, sort of. And he came to visit me but when he found out I kissed him…" I point to Nathan, "he left and stayed with him…" I point to Tarik. "My best friend is here for stakeout purposes and moral support," I say as I point to Jessica (who has taken off her hat), "and I have another friend in the getaway car over there," I say, pointing to the car.

By this time a large crowd has gathered around us and I think a photographer from the campus newspaper just took a picture of us. When my parents find out about this, I'm probably going to be grounded for life.

"Let me get this straight. This guy in handcuffs is your sort-of boyfriend. And you kissed that guy bleeding on the ground over there."

"Yep."

"And none of you are students at Northwestern?"

I nod enthusiastically and say, "You got it." No need to needlessly involve the innocent bystander, Tarik.

The security guys look over at Nathan. "Sir, would you like to press charges against anyone here for assaulting you?"

Nathan looks at Avi and says, "I don't think so."

"Does *anyone* here want to press charges?"

We're all silent.

He walks over to Avi. "Sir, turn around so I can release you from those handcuffs."

"Um…I'd like to keep them on," Avi says.

The security guard puts his fingers to his temples and starts rubbing as if he's got a migraine. "Well, then, whoever is not a student at this school should leave University property as soon as you get this all straightened out." I hear the guy mumbling about crazy teenagers as he walks away and tries to disperse the gaping crowd.

Out of the corner of my eye I spot Miranda stumbling out of my car to join us. But I'm not really focused on her; I'm concentrating on Avi…his eyes piercing mine as we stand by the Northwestern dorm with people watching and Nathan bleeding and Tarik all confused and Jess primping and Miranda trying to look innocent.

Avi's hands are pinned behind his back, still bound by the toy handcuffs. "What now?" he asks me. I've missed his deep, sexy voice.

I lick my lips nervously. "Well, the plan was to kidnap you."

"It was Amy's scatterbrained plan," Nathan chimes in while working his jaw back and forth. "I had nothing to do with it."

"Me, either," Miranda says, standing behind Nathan for protection.

I roll my eyes. My accomplices are such weak sauce.

Jessica, who is now fluffing her hair up, says to Tarik, "I suppose you're Tarik."

He holds out a hand to her. "And you're?"

"Amy's best friend Jessica. But everyone calls me Jess. And that's Nathan and Miranda."

Tarik looks at me, his eyes smiling but his words serious. "What are you planning on doing with him?"

"Do you care?" I ask.

Tarik shrugs. "I might. Then again, I might not."

"Whatever you're going to do," Avi says, "do it. If you haven't realized it, I'm standing handcuffed in the middle of the school campus and people are staring."

Tarik jangles keys from his fingers. "Amy, why don't I take your friends back home while you two work out…whatever you need to work out."

"Really?" I say, giving him my best impression of a thankful puppy dog.

"But if he ends up floating in Lake Michigan tomorrow, I'm not covering for you."

Leaning forward, I kiss Tarik on the cheek and whisper in his ear, "You're a good friend."

After saying my thank-yous to my accomplices and assuring them they'll be well taken care of by Tarik, I grasp Avi's elbow like a police officer would and lead him to the car.

When we reach the car, I open the door for him and gesture toward the seat.

"Aren't you going to take the cuffs off before I get in?"

"Nope."

27

Freedom.

Does it mean freedom from persecution?

Freedom to do whatever you want?

Or is freedom a state of mind?

Maybe it's all of those mixed together.

"You don't trust me?"

I give a short laugh. "I didn't cause that whole scene just to let you go free. Get in."

He bends his head, his hands still bound behind his back, and sits in the passenger seat. He's forced to situate himself so he's not leaning against the uncomfortable cuffs, which makes me want to unshackle him, but what if he decides to leave me after I free him? No, I need him to hear me out, no matter what.

I have to lean over him to put his seatbelt on. He can't do it himself while his hands are bound behind his back. I can feel his breath on my neck as I reach over his body to fasten the seatbelt. It's the law, you know. I think I just heard him give a little grunt/moan combination, but I'm not sure.

"Are you wearing a new perfume?" he asks, his breath hot on my skin. "You smell different."

I don't answer, although it's either the French fries I had at lunch or the Pleasure perfume I sprayed on an hour ago.

"Where are we going?" he asks when I drive off campus, heading north on Sheridan Road.

"You're my prisoner. Prisoners aren't usually told where they're going to be held hostage. And they don't talk." To be honest, I don't know where I'm headed. Somewhere we can be alone, somewhere nobody can find us. If there was a button I could press to whisk us away to a stranded island, I'd do it. He needs to hear me out. After that, well...I'll hold my breath while I wait for his response.

When I reach a red light, I look over at him. He's wearing a gray long-sleeve T-shirt with some logo in Hebrew on it, along with faded jeans with a small rip on one of the knees. I wonder if that rip happened tonight when Nathan jumped him. I can't read Avi's face; he's a master at hiding emotion. Is that something he's been taught, or was he born with that talent?

"Amy, you don't have to do all this," he says.

"Oh, yes. I do," I tell him before I push on the accelerator and start driving again.

"Listen, Amy, when I came to Chicago I didn't know—"

"Avi, wait until you hear me out before you say anything. Okay? I mean, I have some things I have to get off my chest before you tell me how much of a mistake it was that you came here and you're going back home in two days never to see me again."

"Whatever you want," he says, looking out the window and taking a deep, frustrated breath.

Oh, great. Now I've pissed him off. I'm passing the Baha'i Temple, which looks like the Planetarium. It's so huge and brilliantly lit up.

"It's the Baha'i temple," I explain when Avi's eyes go wide from seeing such a unique building.

"Whoa," Avi says. "The one in Haifa by my aunt's house has a gold dome. Stuck in the middle of the mountain you can see it from miles away."

I drive past the temple, past Gillson Park, past the million dollar houses on Sheridan Road *only people who have old money can afford*, my mom says. By the time we pass Glencoe I know my destination.

Rosewood Beach.

It's a small beach in Highland Park my mom took me to one summer when I was little. I remember the wind was so strong my blanket flew up and threw sand in my face. I wasn't a sand person to begin with. It was too messy and got all over and it took days to get out of my hair and shoes. And as much as my mom wanted to get me in that Lake Michigan water, I resisted. I saw the kids who played with their buckets in the water and splashed around…eventually they had to come out of the water and walk on the sand. That dry sand stuck to their feet and legs and hands and…ugh, all over.

Turning into the little driveway leading down to the tiny parking lot, I think of how messy situations can sometimes be a good thing. I think I'm just learning that.

I park the car in the darkened parking lot right near the edge of the beach overlooking the lake. No other car is in sight. We're the only ones here in this secluded place.

Almost as if we're on an island alone.

"Are you going to take the cuffs off now?" he asks.

"Nope. Not until you hear what I have to say." I turn in my seat so I'm facing him. The only thing between us is the arm rest and cup holders. And our strained relationship, if you want to get technical.

I reach over and unbuckle his seatbelt, the click releasing him from the harness. He's as comfortable as he's gonna get with his hands secured behind his back.

His eyes are shining in the bright moonlight. I can feel them on me as though they were his hands.

"Don't look at me," I tell him.

"Why not?"

"It embarrasses me. What I'm about to say embarrasses me."

"So let me talk," he says in his smooth, confident voice. "I'm not embarrassed."

I tilt my head and raise my eyebrows. "Just turn around."

He shakes his head in confusion, but turns and stares out the opposite window.

I brace myself for the worst and start talking. "Last

summer was the best summer of my life. Meeting someone I really liked surprised me more than anything."

"Same here," he says to the window.

"Yeah, but you told me not to wait for you. You didn't want to get involved, you didn't want a relationship…all you wanted was a summer fling."

"It was awesome."

"Yeah. But then it was over. You went to the army and I came back home. When things go wrong with Jess, I can't call you. When things go wrong with friends at school or my family, you're not here to calm me down and tell me not to freak out or hold my hand in that familiar way."

This time he turns to me, his jaw clenched. "So you replaced me with Nathan?"

With my index finger, I twirl it in cirlces to remind him to turn around.

He looks at the window again and repeats, "So you replaced me with Nathan. I get it, Amy, you don't have to state the obvious."

"I admit it," I say quietly. "I kissed Nathan. Twice. And he was a good kisser. Well, the first time he wasn't, but the second time was considerably better."

"I don't want to hear it," Avi says, his voice tight.

"Yes, you do. I don't want secrets between us, Avi. And I don't want you running away from me when things get tough."

"I don't run."

"You left so fast I didn't have a chance to figure things out in my own head," I say, putting my hand on his thigh.

I need to touch him, to make him realize how much I care. Will he know by my touch how much I want him back in my life, how there's a void in my heart only he can fill?

He looks down at my hand. "Did you figure it out?"

"I didn't kidnap you for nothing, you know. Stay with me, Avi. Stick with me through my mistakes and through my crap and through my crabbiness and through my doubts because…oh, God, I love you."

I'm waiting for him to say it back to me, not that it even matters. My love won't waver. I can list one reason, or a hundred reasons, why I love him. There's a connection when we laugh, when we fight, and when we kiss…there's a restlessness that burns inside me for him when he's not with me. I'm calmer when we're together.

He's in the Israeli army, I know. And I won't likely be seeing him for a long time. Maybe he'll get leave in the summer; maybe he won't. It doesn't even matter to me, as long as we take the time now to say whatever, whenever.

"Come here," he says.

I look over at the small space in the front seat, the cup holders and arm rest between us. "Um, where do you want me to go, Avi? There's not much room here."

"You're smart. Figure it out."

Don't ask me how it is that my prisoner is giving me the orders now, but I'm totally okay with it. I squeeze my way over the hump of the armrest and wiggle my way over to the passenger side, finally able to sit comfortably while straddling his legs.

"I'm selfish," Avi says, his dark chocolate eyes boring

into mine. "Because I don't want to share you." He bends his head down, says something in Hebrew to himself that sounds like a curse, and says, "My ego took a beating when I found out you kissed Nathan. I left you because my damn ego was bruised."

I twist my head down so he can see my face. "If you can forgive me, I can forgive you…and your ego," I say. "I just want to spend every second together before you go back to Israel."

"And after I go back, what's between us? I've got three years in the army. Who knows what'll happen."

"I don't want to break up, Avi."

"Me, either. How about a don't ask, don't tell relationship until I'm out of the army?"

Don't ask, don't tell. That sounds fair. "Sababa. Does that mean I can call you my boyfriend instead of my *non*-boyfriend?"

The side of his mouth quirks up. "Definitely."

"Do we have a contract drawn up? Do we shake on it?"

"How about we seal the deal with a kiss. No distractions this time."

We both lean forward, meeting in the middle. Just as our lips are about to touch, my cell phone rings.

"Aren't you going to get it? It might be your dad."

Tilting my head to the side and brushing my lips against his, I say, "No distractions, remember?"

Ignoring the persistent phone, we start kissing softly, the way it was the first time he ever touched me. Sweet and slow, with passion and hunger lurking behind as if waiting to be unleashed with a vengeance.

Lips against lips, I caress his face before moving my hands down to the hard planes of his chest, exploring my way while he's still bound and we're still kissing.

"One day we're going to do this somewhere else than in a car," he says, his voice and breath coming harder than before. Through his shirt I can feel his heart racing faster, too. I smile, knowing that I can bring him to feel this way, that he wants me as much as I want him.

Wiggling closer to him and putting the seat into a reclining position, I realize I'm playing with fire but it feels too good to stop. Groaning sounds fill the car. I'm not even sure if they're coming from me or him. Avi nuzzles my neck with his lips, licking and kissing a path down to the V in my shirt while my fingers are wandering around his body giving caresses of their own.

With a shift of his body, suddenly Avi's hands are on my waist, moving up my spine and cradling my head. His breathing is heavy and erratic and his eyes are so intense when he looks into mine it makes my breath hitch.

"You're free from the handcuffs?" I whisper, feeling weak from his kisses and caresses and hands and words.

Between kissing me, he says, "Yeah. There was a release button on them."

I lean back, separating our lips and bodies for a second. "When did you find it?"

"About ten seconds after you put them on me." His fingers brush stray strands of hair away from my face. "The funny thing is, you don't need handcuffs to bind me to you. I'm yours without them."

I pull his head toward mine, and we kiss and continue exploring as we move in rhythm against each other.

"I want to forget how inexperienced you are," he groans the words into my ear.

"So teach me," I say. I bite my lower lip as I sit up and unbutton the top two buttons of my shirt.

"Look at me?" Avi asks.

"Why?"

"So I can see your eyes."

Avi's eyes are totally focused on my face and not my shirt as I move my hands lower and start unbuttoning the rest of the buttons. My hands are shaking. I'm not sure if it's from the cold car or my trembling nerves.

"Didn't you listen when your dad had the sex talk? Didn't he tell you boys only want one thing?"

"Do you, Avi? Do you only want one thing?" I say as I open my shirt and reveal my bra beneath it.

"To be honest, my body's only thinking about one thing right now."

"Me, too. Aren't you going to take your shirt off?"

As his hands reach for the hem of his shirt he says in a strained voice, "Your dad's gonna kill me," then he lifts his shirt over his head and tosses it onto the drivers seat with his eyes never leaving me.

Brushing the tips of his fingers across my abdomen, my body tingles in response and I shiver. "Are you okay with this?" he asks, his face serious.

I nod and give him a small smile. "I'll let you know when I'm not."

As I lean down to press our bodies against each other, his hands reach around under my open shirt and pull me toward him. "Your body...so warm."

His hands are like a fire, consuming my body with his touch. I lean my head on his chest, hearing his heart beating in the same erratic rhythm as my own while his hands move up and caress my hair, my bare back, and my breasts.

I reclaim his lips and my raw emotions and new wonderful feelings whirl in my consciousness. I'm fully aware I'm not ready to have sex, but I'm ready to experience more... "Avi," I say, letting my tone say more than my words. I want...

As if he understands, Avi shifts again, this time moving our bodies so he's on top of me. "Ow," he says.

"What?" Did I do something to hurt him?

"I just banged my head on the mirror."

"I think the seatbelt is digging into my back," I tell him. Or maybe it's the handcuffs digging into my back. Or both. All I know is that we're both uncomfortable right now.

He puts his forehead against mine and groans in frustration as he attempts to stretch his legs out so they're not pinning mine under his. I think one of his legs is under the steering wheel, but I can't be sure.

My hands are on his shoulders, my feet scrunched

under the dashboard, and I think Avi's elbow is stuck in the cup holder.

And now my cell phone is ringing again.

"This isn't working, is it?" he says.

I scan our position, the awkwardness of it all. "I guess you're right," I say, totally frustrated.

He leans into the back seat, retrieves the ringing phone, and hands it to me.

Flipping it open, I say, "Hey, *Aba.*"

Avi twists himself and ends up sitting in the driver's seat.

"Are you okay?" my dad barks on the other end of the line.

"Yeah." More than okay.

"Then I'm going to kill you. Where are you? I've been calling and calling. Why get you a cell phone if you won't answer it?"

"I didn't hear the phone," I lie, interrupting his tirade. "I must have been in a bad cell area." That is such a lame answer, but I'm not too good at coming up with lies on the fly.

"Where are you? I asked Nathan, but he's keeping his lips tighter than a submarine door. Are you in some kind of trouble?"

"I'm with Avi," I finally say while tossing the handcuffs into the back seat so they're not pressing into my back anymore.

"I thought he went to stay with his friend at Northwestern. You told me it was over between you two."

"It was…but not anymore. He's coming back home to

stay with us." I say the words, then look over at Avi hoping he'll agree to sleep at our condo tonight and every night until his plane leaves.

"Are you with him now?"

"Yes."

"Alone?"

I look out over the empty parking lot, the deserted beach, and the frozen Lake Michigan water glittering in the moonlight. "Yes," I say.

"Put Avi on the phone. Right. Now."

"*Aba*, don't embarrass me."

"Let me tell you this much, Amy. If you don't put him on the phone, I'm taking away your cell phone, your computer privileges, car privileges, and that boy is not allowed in my home. Got it?"

My dad is a total buzz kill. I hold out the phone to Avi. "He wants to talk to you."

Avi takes the phone with all seriousness. "*Ken*," he says. Yes.

I only hear Avi's part of the conversation, but it doesn't even matter because he's in full-blown Hebrew mode.

"*Ani shomer aleha. Ken. He beseder. Ken, ani rotze lishmor al kol chelkay hagouf sheli.*"

"What's he saying?" I whisper.

Avi holds his hand over the mouthpiece. "He's going through a list of my body parts he'll rearrange if I 'compromise' you."

I slap my hand over my eyes. Seriously, my dad could

drive any guy away from me, even a commando in the Israel Defense Forces.

"Ron, *ta'ameen li…ani ohev et habat shelcha ve lo ya'aseh cloom lif'goah bah.*"

After Avi said that last part, there's silence on the other end of the line for a second. I can feel the tension ebb and flow between the two men in my life.

"*Beseder,*" Avi says.

"*Beseder,*" he repeats.

"*Beseder,*" he says again.

The suspense is killing me. "What does *beseder* mean?"

Instead of answering me, he collapses the phone, disconnecting the line. Then he tosses the phone into the back seat. "It means 'fine', or 'okay.'"

"Did he really threaten you?"

"Especially after I told him I loved you."

Heart palpitation here. "You told him you loved me?"

He nods.

I tilt my head to the side and say with a smile, "You know you're supposed to declare your love to the girl before you tell her father. Unless it's the olden days, in which you'd be giving my dad goats, gifts, and gold in exchange for permission to marry me."

"My family owns half of the goats on the *moshav,*" he says, lifting his eyebrows. "How about I offer our half to your dad?"

I was at the *moshav* over the summer. My uncle owns

the other half of the goat farm. "That's a lot of goats," I say. "How do you know I'm worth it?"

Avi looks into my eyes. "You're worth it, Amy," he says, once again cradling my head in his hands. "Trust me, life with you would be an adventure," he whispers.

As I'm about to pull him closer, I feel him tugging my shirt together. "What are you doing?"

"Buttoning your shirt," he says as his hands deftly move up and button my shirt back up.

"Why?"

"Because I'd rather have you not tell our kids their dad declared his love in the back seat of a car."

"We're in the front seat."

"Yeah, well…and as much as I think I could take your dad on and give him a pretty good run for his money, I'd rather not get into it with him."

Avi puts his own shirt on, covering that six-pack and bronzed chest I once thought didn't affect me. It does.

"Let's take a walk on the beach."

I look out the window and know it's a cold, breezy night in northern Illinois. "It's freezing out there."

"Stay close, then. I'll keep you warm."

We step out of the car. Avi puts his arm around me as we walk down the dark, sandy beach. He's right. His embrace does keep me warm on this chilly night. After a few minutes, Avi halts his steps and turns to me. He takes my hands in his, weaving my fingers through his own. "Amy," he says, his voice laced with seriousness.

My eyes are filled with emotion. He's going to say it…I know it's so hard for him. His brother died in a bombing and Avi's been struggling with his emotions ever since.

He squeezes his eyes shut as if trying desperately to pull out the words. "Wait here." Taking my car keys from his back pocket, he runs to the car and back. "Here," he says, holding out my cell phone. "Call your voicemail."

"Why?"

"Just do it."

I dial my voicemail number. The first call was from five o'clock…before I kidnapped him.

"Hi, Amy, it's Avi. I've, uh, been thinking a lot this week and the truth is…well, I miss you. Too much. It's killing me inside not being close to you. I mean, I understand if you want to never call or see me again because I left like a wounded ass, but…well…if you find it in your heart…or even your mind…to forgive me for having an ego as big as the Sears Tower I visited yesterday, call me back on this number – it's Tarik's cell."

I press nine on my cell and turn to him. "That was so sweet," I say. And it means so much to me that he called before I kidnapped him.

"Wait, listen to the next message."

The next message? I put my ear back on the phone to hear the next message.

"It's Avi again. Did I tell you your eyes remind me of blown glass? I can see your soul through those eyes, Amy. They get darker when you're trying to be sexy and they shine when

237

you smile. And when you think you're in trouble you blink double the amount that you usually do. And when you're sad, the corners of your eyes turn down. I miss your eyes. And I don't want the sad ones to be my last memory of you."

I save the second message, too, then look up at Avi. "There's another one, isn't there?"

He nods.

I press the button and forward to the next message.

"*It's Avi. And I want to say something to you. Not because I want you to say it back, either.* (deep breath*) I…I love you. It's not that kind of conditional love…it's the kind that'll be around forever. Even if you don't call. Even if you like Nathan or any other guy. We can be friends. We can be more. Just…call me back.*"

I press the forward button. Avi looks like he wants to bite his nails right now, he's so embarrassed.

"*Did I mention when I first met you I was so attracted to you it scared me? Me, scared. I still am when I'm around you, because now I want you in my life forever. How long is forever, Amy?*"

I shut the phone off.

"Don't you want to hear the rest of the messages?"

I slip the phone into my back pocket while tears well in my eyes. "No." Well, actually I'll listen to them when I'm alone in my room at night and want to hear his voice before I fall asleep. Right now all I want to do is be with my boyfriend and enjoy the small amount of time we have left with each other.

"Avi?"

"Yeah."

"Now I have to tell our kids you declared your love over a cell phone."

He smiles wide, then laughs. "How about this, then…" he says, then picks me up effortlessly in his strong arms and lays me gently down on the sand.

I have to say, I'm much less worried about the sand in my hair or stuck to my designer clothes than the words about to come out of Avi's mouth.

He leans over me. His hands once again take mine in his and he weaves his fingers through mine. "I love you, Amy Nelson-Barak. From the moment I laid eyes on you I couldn't stop looking at you. From the moment we talked I couldn't stop arguing with you. From the moment we kissed I couldn't stop kissing you. And from the moment we shared our hopes, fears, and insecurities I couldn't stop loving you."

Oh, that's good. Twice.

Is today Tuesday?

28

King Solomon didn't ask God to be rich or to live long. He asked for wisdom and knowledge (Kings 3:9). I have to be honest…I'm more selfish than King Solomon. Abercrombie & Fitch is having a sale next week and, well…

It's after midnight when we get back to my condo. We had to retrieve Avi's duffle from Tarik's dorm at Northwestern before coming back home where my dad has been waiting for us like an overprotective lion waiting for his precious cub to return from her first hunt.

My dad situated one of our dining room chairs right in front of the door so his face is the first thing we see. His hair is all messed up, no doubt from running his hands through it a million times.

"Hey, *Aba*," I say, giving him a peck on his cheek while trying to keep the atmosphere light. Mutt jumps over to me, totally excited and wagging his tail furiously. I pet him, then look back at my stoic dad.

His eyes are narrowed at Avi, who is standing in the doorway with his duffle in hand.

Showdown time.

I put my purse on the table, wondering how long these two can stare each other down. "Avi, why don't you come in while I get the sheets for your bed."

Avi looks to my dad for approval. Oh, no. I seriously think my dad might just kick him out right now.

Is anyone else going to talk? Or are the two guys going to stand here staring each other down until one of them gives in and looks away? They're like dogs.

"If you loved my daughter you'd have her home at a decent hour."

Avi opens his mouth as if he's going to say something back, but then closes it. My dad seems content with the silence coming from Avi, as if he's not even expecting a response. I go to the hall closet to get the sheets because I'm too embarrassed to witness my dad going off on my boyfriend and know I can't stop it from happening.

When I walk back into the living room, the scene has changed. Avi is sitting on the couch while my dad has moved the dining room chair into the living room. He's sitting in the chair, facing Avi and watching him.

While Avi and I arrange the sheets, my dad doesn't change expression or flinch. When I hand Avi a pillow and our hands lightly brush against each other, I wonder if my dad can tell how electric that instantaneous touch was.

As soon as the couch is transformed into a bed, my dad barks, "Time for bed."

I change into pj's in my room and pass Avi in the hallway when I go to the bathroom to brush my teeth and wash my face. Looking at myself in the mirror, I see a happy person who's content with her life. It's not perfect, that's for sure. But I'm getting there.

Stepping out of the bathroom, I notice my dad has moved the chair from the living room into the hallway, directly between my room and the living room where Avi is sleeping.

"*Aba*, how long are you going to be sitting there?" I ask him.

"All night."

I can't even get mad at him. I know he just worries about me and questions his own effectiveness as a father. After all, I've only lived with him a few months and he's still getting used to having a teenage daughter around. He's probably wondering what to tell my mom if she grills him on my life. Considering last year I didn't even want to talk to him, I understand why he's sitting on a chair in the middle of the hallway and isn't willing to budge anytime soon.

Moving past him, I say, "I just want to say goodnight to Avi. Does that meet with your approval?"

"That depends on how long your goodnight will last," he says, abandoning his post to follow me.

Okay, so three's a crowd in this scenario. It's not easy

saying goodnight to the guy of your dreams when your dad is standing over your shoulder.

"Well, goodnight Avi," I say sheepishly when I get to the living room and wish we were still on the beach…without an overprotective chaperone.

Avi is sitting on the sofa, wearing baggy shorts and…well, that's about it. As much as I hate people staring at my chest, I have the hardest time not staring at his. I think he sits there half-dressed to tempt me.

Two can play at this game.

I can't do it now, but tomorrow I'm going to taunt him by wearing something extra low-cut and tight. Let's see how he reacts in the morning.

He's got this huge grin on his face. He has no clue I have ideas spinning in my head. "*Lyla tov*, Amy," he says, telling me goodnight in his native language.

I want to say more, but not with my bodyguard behind me, so I stroll back to my room. Although, one backward glance at Avi and I know I don't even have to say the words. He knows how I feel and what I want to say.

"Seriously, *Aba*, do you know how embarrassed you're making me?"

"Seriously, Amy, do you know I don't care?"

I roll my eyes. In bed, I wonder how long he'll stay perched on that chair in the middle of the hallway. I hope he falls asleep in that chair and gets a crick in his neck.

I cuddle under the covers of my bed, wishing I was cuddling with Avi instead of my Care Bear.

Two more nights until Avi leaves. How is my heart not going to crush into a million pieces? And how am I going to sleep tonight when I'm too excited to go to bed? I'm replaying the evening in my head, focusing on the "I love you" parts and conveniently skipping over the embarrassing parts on the Northwestern campus.

Because that can easily be erased from my memory.

Although…I wonder if Jess, Nathan, and Miranda are okay. If you want to get technical about it, I did ditch them tonight.

29

Sarah gave birth to Isaac when she was ninety years old and her husband, Abraham, was one hundred years old (Genesis 17:17). I hope my mom and Marc aren't going to keep having kids until they're that old.

I love weekends. Especially when I don't have any homework and my boyfriend is in town.

In the morning, I walk out of my bedroom wearing a black, extra-small wrap shirt that shows off way too much cleavage. Jess and I both bought one last winter when they were the hottest fashion, but we were too embarrassed to wear them in public.

During breakfast, I make a big production out of bending down to pour Avi cereal. He's not looking; every time I check his eyes are focused on his food. I keep bringing him stuff…bread, hummus, orange juice. He looks at my face, but definitely not my cleavage. What's up with that?

When my dad walks into the kitchen, he takes one

look at me and slaps his hands over his eyes. "Amy, where's the rest of your shirt?"

"This is it."

"Um…no. No. No. No. It doesn't cover your…parts." He points to Avi. "Close your eyes." He shakes the same finger at me, but still has one hand over his eyes. "Go back in your room and put on something VERY conservative. That covers those girl things."

Avi's shoulders are shaking and I think he just spit out his cereal from trying to cover up his laughter.

I huff in frustration and look at my boyfriend. "Did you not notice my boobs practically hanging out?"

Avi looks from me to my dad. "Um…is this a talk we should be having in front of your *aba*?"

My dad holds up his hands, stopping the conversation. "This is a conversation that should not be happening *at all*. Amy, I'm calling your mom. *After* you change your shirt. This is out of my jurisdiction."

I change, then have to deal with my mom and dad talking on the phone about me for fifteen minutes.

"I noticed them, Amy," Avi says as I plunk myself back down at the kitchen table.

"Well, you weren't staring at 'em," I say accusingly.

"I didn't know you wanted me to."

He's got me there. Usually I hate people staring at my over-abundance of frontage that God "blessed me with" (my mom's phrase, not mine). Avi knows this. I know I'm being ridiculous and not making any sense.

"If it makes you feel any better, when you turned away I couldn't take my eyes off them."

Even though I know this entire conversation is ridiculous, I say, "Thank you, Avi."

He gives me one of his signature half-smiles. "It's all sababa."

"Yeah," I say. "It is."

After my mom has a "talk" with me over the phone about private parts remaining private, I drag Avi to the Museum of Science and Industry. It's my favorite museum, especially the dead baby exhibit. Okay, so technically it's called the neonatal exhibit, showcasing embryos and fetuses in formaldehyde. I've always been fascinated with the exhibit: seeing how human life starts as a speck and ends up a real person. Total miracle, I can't describe it any other way.

Makes you believe in God all over again.

I thought Avi would be bored looking at the dead babies, but when I glance over at him and catch him riveted to the exhibit I know he feels the same way about it that I do. As I study the stages of development, my heart goes out to the mothers of these children who weren't able to grow up. They lost their lives before life even started. But they're doing more for people than most do in a lifetime, surely more than I've done in my seventeen years. They've made people more educated, they've made people aware of what it's like inside of a woman's body as she's pregnant with a child, and they even bring people closer to God.

Avi takes my hand in his as we stop at each stage of development and study the fetuses. They're labeled as male or female (even identical twins are labeled) and how many weeks old they are.

Avi puts his hand up to the glass, right in front of the fetus that looks fully developed except it's so small. "I've never seen anything like this," he says.

I know it's not everyone's favorite exhibit, and if you really think about it it's kind of creepy. But it makes me feel good knowing I've shared it with Avi and he appreciates it as much as I do. Maybe one day…

I look over at Avi. He smiles. I can tell he's thinking the same thing.

In the afternoon, I take him along with Mutt to my mom's house. I can't have Avi go back to Israel without meeting the other half of my nuclear family, although I'm not sure how Marc and Mom will act around him. And now that we've just seen the neonatal exhibit at the Museum of Science and Industry, I hope my mom being pregnant doesn't freak Avi out.

As soon Mom sees Mutt, she says, "Do you have to bring the animal?" she says.

"Mom, you have a yard he can run in. He loves your yard."

Since I'm keeping Mutt on an extender leash at the park so he doesn't impregnate anyone else's dog, my mom's place is like Freedom City for him.

"Last time you didn't pick up all of his poop, Amy. Marc stepped in a little present last week."

Way to go, Mutt! "Sorry, Mom," I try and say sincerely, although in the back of my head I think God had something to do with it. *B'shert*, right? Meant to be.

"Amy, don't tell me you're sorry. Tell Marc."

After I let Mutt loose in the backyard, my mom says, "I'm going to assume you're Avi."

Avi gives her one of his killer smiles, putting on the Avi charm, and shakes her hand. My heart flips over because I know he's doing it for me, that it's important to him that my mom likes him. And maybe because he's lost some brownie points with my dad after last night and he wants to rack some up with my mom before he leaves. Smart guy.

"So, how old are you again?" Mom asks as she pats down her model blonde hair. If I didn't know better, I'd think my mom was trying to rack up brownie points with Avi.

Amy, don't go off on her. She's not embarrassing you on purpose. Wait to interfere when she pulls out the naked baby pictures.

"Eighteen," Avi replies.

"And you're in the Israeli army?"

"Yes."

My mom sits down at the kitchen table and says, "So…what do you do there?"

"Mom, he's training to be a commando," I say, interrupting. "He can't tell you what he does all day."

"Do you shoot guns?"

Avi looks from me to my mom and back. "When we have to," he says.

I need a Coke. This is harder than I thought. I open the refrigerator, but there's no Coke…no Diet Coke, no Cherry Coke, no Vanilla Coke. There's not even a Coke Zero. "Uh, Mom, where's the Coke?"

"We don't have any in the house. It's not good for the baby," she says, then touches her stomach.

As I stare at her hand caressing her abdomen, I think about the neonatal exhibit we saw today. For the first time, I can picture what my little brother or sister looks like right now. The size of my fist…or maybe even smaller.

Marc stumbles into the kitchen, introduces himself to Avi, and the two shake hands. "Do you play golf?" Marc asks, then sneezes into a handkerchief he just pulled from his pocket.

"No. Soccer's my sport," Avi says, then looks to me. I shrug, confused. Does Marc want to go hit a few at the range with Avi to test his skill with a club? Or is he desperately trying to have a manly sports conversation or, scarier yet, a sports competition?

"Why don't you boys see if there's a soccer game on TV while Amy helps me set the table?"

"I can help, too," Avi says.

"Go ahead," I say and push him gently out of the kitchen. I need private time to gossip about him with my mom.

While Marc and Avi settle into the living room, my mom and I set the table. Mom is smiling wide and staring at me as if I just got engaged or something. "He's adorable," she says. "I can see how you can be so hung up on him."

Hung up on him? I'm a little more than hung up on him, I'm full blown *in love* with the guy and even being one room away I realize is too far for me. I don't even want to think about tomorrow, when I have to drive him to the airport and watch a plane taking off with him inside.

Staring at the fresh flowers in the middle of the kitchen table, I say, "Mom, how many times have you been in love?"

"How many times did I *think* I was in love or how many times have I *really* been in love?"

"How do you know the difference?"

"You don't. Well, not at the time you're having the feelings. I was in love with Danny Peterson in high school; we dated my junior and senior year."

"What happened with Danny?"

"I caught him kissing Shayna Middleton under the bleachers during gym class. Guess he didn't love me as much as I loved him. Then there was your dad."

Deep in my mom's blue eyes I detect sadness. "Why didn't you marry him, Mom? I know he wanted to marry you, but you wouldn't."

She wrings her hands together on the table. "My parents...your grandparents...they didn't think your father was good for me. He was a foreigner, someone who might leave me and go back to Israel or who knows where. Or marry me just for citizenship and leave me."

"Do you wish things were different?" I ask. I mean, if she married my dad when she got pregnant then I wouldn't have to deal with a sneezing stepdad and my parents wouldn't live miles away from each other. We'd be a whole family, not a broken one.

She says softly, "To be honest…no. It would have never worked between your father and me. He's married to his work, and I need a man who'll pay attention to me. Marc maneuvers his work schedule around me, not the other way around."

A little piece of hope in my chest disappears with her words. Every birthday I prayed my parents would get together—every penny I threw into fountains, every time I blew an eyelash off of my finger. Now I realize all the hoping and praying wasn't going to change the course of things. There are some things I can't change, after all.

"Do you wish you'd never had me?" I say with a lump in my throat.

Her eyes go wide, "No! Amy, I wouldn't change having you for anything in the world."

"Mom, I was a mistake. Face it, you didn't mean to get pregnant in college on a one-night stand."

"Let's just say you weren't expected. But there was no way I was giving you up and when I held you in my arms the first time after giving birth to you, I cried so hard…from happiness, Amy. Because I'd never known how much I wanted you until I held you. From that moment on, you had my heart. I know I haven't been the best mom. I've grown up while raising you and made many mistakes."

We all make mistakes. "I have, too." But I'm trying to mend them.

Will my dad ever maneuver his work around a woman? Yeah, maybe when he's a hundred years old and is forced to slow down. I need to find out why he works so much, what drives him to put his personal life second to his work life.

"I'm sorry, Amy," Mom says, giving me a puppy dog look Mutt would be proud of. "I wish I could have given you the family you've always wanted."

I smile warmly and stop her hands from wringing by putting my hands over hers. "It's okay, Mom. For the first time in my life, I understand."

Dinner with my mom and Marc was nice. Since we couldn't have sushi because of my mom's pregnancy, we ordered Thai instead. Marc tried to engage Avi in conversation, but Marc isn't the most interesting person to chat with. Get him on a subject he knows, though, and he's a maniac. Like real estate. He could talk about prime Chicago real estate for hours. It's too bad nobody wants to listen.

After dinner Avi and I get in the car and cruise back to the city.

"Are we going back to the beach?" he asks. "Because I think another late night like yesterday and your dad really will pull out the Uzi."

"What's an Uzi?"

"An Israeli-made machine gun. Very popular during your dad's time in the military."

Yeah, I can see it. My dad waiting at the door sitting in the dining room chair with an Israeli machine gun strapped to his shoulder instead of just an angry stare.

"Nope. I'm taking you to a club. You took me to a club in Israel. It's time for me to show you what clubs are like here."

"I thought you had to be twenty-one to get into clubs in the States."

"Yeah, well, this one is lenient. Besides, I know the guy playing in the band."

30

> *Abraham had such faith and fear in God he almost*
> *sacrificed his son Isaac because God commanded it*
> *(Genesis 22:2). Abraham knew God would make*
> *everything okay in the end. I have faith that God will*
> *make everything okay in the end, too.*

We wait in line to get into Durty Nevin's until Jess pulls us out of line and leads us to the front door. She mumbles something about her uncle being part owner of the security company responsible for the bouncers. We walk straight up to the burly bouncer, he takes one look at Jess, and waves the three of us in.

I hold Avi's hand as we weave through the sea of people.

Miranda is sitting at a table up front. She's wearing her hair up in a ponytail and has actual makeup on. "Wow, Miranda, you look great!" I say to her.

The girl smiles as if I just told her she won a million-dollar lottery. "Jess did it for me."

I give Jess a thumbs-up sign, then join the others to snatch chairs for the three of us.

As soon as we sit, I reach for Avi's hand. His hand is already reaching for mine. Looking up, I swallow hard when he flashes me a private knowing wink.

"I'm glad you two worked it out, but if you start any major PDA I swear I'm banning you from this table," Jess says, eyeing our hands.

"What's PDA?" Avi says in my ear. Jess rolls her eyes, thinking he's whispering about how much he loves me and adores me and can't live without me.

I lean toward him, my hand braced on his chest as I whisper back, "Public display of affection. You know, making out in front of everyone."

Jess is pulling me off him. "I need to talk to you, Amy. It's important. If you could separate yourself from your man for one second, that is."

Tossing Avi an apologetic expression, I pry myself away and let Jessica pull me by my elbow into the hallway by the bathrooms. Music is blaring and pounding in my ears, but it sounds good. Anything would sound good to me right now. I'm happy.

Jess is flushed as she stops and faces me. This is serious. I can tell by the way her mouth and stance get all intense and stiff. "I'm in love, Amy. And I know it sounds weird and I don't want to get all dorky and googly-eyed like you and Avi, but I know he's 'The One.' And my parents are going to have a complete meltdown when they meet him because he's everything they've ever wanted for me. He's Jewish, he's Israeli, he's gorgeous, intelligent, he's sweeter than a cinnamon bun…he's every Jewish parent's wet dream—"

I put a hand up, wondering what this is all about. Cinnamon bun? Israeli? *Wet dream?* "Jess, the only Israeli you've been in contact with lately is Avi and my dad. Avi is taken and my dad…" I scrunch up my face in full gross-out mode.

"I'm not in love with your dad, Amy," Jess says, her hands on her hips.

"Phew," I say, physically and mentally relieved. I just saved myself years of therapy.

"I'm in love with Tarik. You know, Avi's friend at Northwestern. After your kidnapping fiasco, he drove Miranda and Nathan home. Then we talked in the car for over an hour in front of my building." I can't stop the girl or get a word in. She's like a train that won't stop. More like a train wreck, because she's totally clueless. I listen to the rest of her rant before breaking the bad news. "He's the smartest guy, Amy. I can't believe you've known him since the summer, knew he was coming to Northwestern, but didn't introduce him to me. I would question your loyalty to me, but I'm so ridiculously in love. Did you ever think I would believe in love at first sight? I swear, I couldn't sleep last night thinking about him and this morning I had the biggest urge to go visit him and surprise him at the dorm. You know the way you feel about Avi? I feel the same way."

"Do you think I could talk now, Jess?" I ask her. She laughs, this crazy I-am-in-love-and-can't-be-normal laugh. Gee, I hope I'm not like that around Avi. Someone slap me please if I ever go over the deep end like that. "What did you guys talk about for an hour?"

"Everything. Life, family, friends."

"Jess, I hate to break it to you, but…" How do I tell her that 1: Love at first sight is a bunch of bull. And 2: He's—

"Wait. Before you tell me I'm crazy and go off on me that I'm supposed to be the friend who is realistic and sane, I need to know his last name. I don't even know my future husband's name."

"Muslim."

Jess cocks her head to the side in confusion. "Tarik Muslim? That's not a Jewish name, that's a religion. Amy, stop making fun of me and tell me his last name before I start getting pissed."

"He's Muslim, Jess," I say slowly with a serious expression on my face. It's really a pity expression, because I'm about to tell her that her cinnamon bun has raisins in it when she expected it to be plain.

"Amy, you said he was Israeli."

"No, I said he was Avi's friend from Israel. So as much as you like him, your parents would freak. Especially your dad. Isn't he the president of the men's club at the synagogue? I admit Tarik is awesome, Jess. But your parents want you to find a nice Jewish boy and I'm sure his parents want him to find a nice Muslim girl."

I shouldn't have put it like that. Just by looking at Jessica I can tell she's gone from elation to confusion to sorrow to defiance all in a matter of seconds. Defiance in my best friend is scary.

"He asked me out on Saturday night," she says matter-of-factly.

Oh, man. "And?"

"And of course I said yes. Crap," she says, as tears start filling her eyes. She turns and hurries into the restroom, leaving me to either go after her like a good friend or pay attention to my boyfriend who probably thinks I ditched him.

I peek around the corner to check out what my boyfriend is doing. He's abandoned the table and is talking to a couple of guys at the bar.

I decide to be a good friend and hope Avi can amuse himself for another five minutes.

In the restroom, Jess has some other girls from our school gathered around her, asking what's wrong. Mitch cruelly dumped her and now the guy of her dreams turns out to be a guy she's probably forbidden to date. Jessica goes to Hebrew school twice a week, Sunday school, and in the summers Jess rides a bus all the way to the middle of Wisconsin to spend four weeks at a Jewish overnight camp.

Needless to say it's been ingrained in Jessica's head

since she was born that she has to marry a Jewish boy. Her kids have to be Jewish, and it's her responsibility to carry on the Jewish traditions and religion.

But I never lose hope. There must be some loophole, some way Tarik and Jess can date without causing her Grandma Pearl to go into a nursing home prematurely.

Jessica waves the crowd away. "I'm fine. Really." She's trying to convince them. It's not working. First of all, her mascara is running down her face like streaks of ash with tears leading the way.

I push everyone else out of the way. Picking her chin up with my fingers, I say quietly, "Jess, don't cry. I'm sure once you explain the situation to your parents, it won't be such a big deal. You'll see."

Leading me to the side, away from everyone else, she says, "No, I won't. My mom's family was killed in the Holocaust, Amy. My great-grandfather has a number tattooed on his arm from when he was in a concentration camp. A reminder you can't wash away with soap and water. If I even mention a non-Jewish boy's name in his presence I feel guilty."

I still think God will take care of Jessica and look after her. I have complete faith. And there's always the guilt offering of a burnt animal...

Jess wipes her eyes, trying to compose herself. Grabbing paper towels and looking into the mirror, she witnesses the streaky mess her face is. "Take a look at me, Amy," she says. "I can't go out there looking like this."

"You have to. Nathan's counting on us being here."

New tears start streaming down her face and she turns to me. "Tarik said he'd be honored to go to the Valentine's Dance with me, Amy. *Honored.* When I spilled the beans about how I didn't have a date, he asked me. Right there in his car in front of my condo. And we had *a moment.* I know it sounds crazy and stupid, but we did."

A moment? Is she kidding me? A moment of lust, perhaps, but not love.

Oh, man. I know how much she wants to go to the Valentine's Dance. It's not about the dance. It's not about love. It's about being wanted and accepted.

I wish I could stop her from looking in the mirror again, but it's no use. One more wipe of the running mascara and I can see the defeat in her eyes. "I'm going home. Tell Nathan and Miranda I'll see them at school."

She moves past me and out the door. I don't even try and stop her because I've been best friends with Jessica long enough to know I can't convince her to stay. Besides, what more can I say? I can't tell her Tarik isn't awesome, because he is.

Speaking of awesome guys, I've left mine alone enough tonight. Heading back to the big crowd, I scan the area and find Avi sitting at the table with Miranda. They're surrounded by a bunch of people, talking and laughing. Two girls who I've never seen before are standing right near Avi. I can tell they're flirting by the way one is flipping her hair and the other girl is licking her lips. My protective radar goes off (okay, my jealousy radar goes off, too) and I weave through the mass of people with my chest held high, and steer toward my boyfriend like a paper clip to a magnet.

The hair-flipping girl is telling a story about her trip to Israel two summers ago and how she's *dying* to go back. It's hard to hear the details of her adventures because music is blaring in the background and I'm stuck standing behind Miranda. There's no room next to my boyfriend.

The lip-licker is laughing while lip-licking, which I think she's practiced in the mirror before. She does it frighteningly well. Avi is so intrigued with her conversation he doesn't know I'm standing here.

Miranda looks up at me. "Maya is telling us about her trip to Israel," Miranda tells me. "She went to *Gadna* for a week. It's a military training camp."

Oh, great. Flippy-haired Maya can talk guns with my commando boyfriend. I'm feeling sick and might just follow Jessica out the door so I can go home, too. "I went to Israel, too," I blurt out.

I have nothing else to say. I didn't go to an Israeli military training camp and I don't have hair I can flip over my shoulder and make it look like I just got it styled at a salon.

When I get Avi's attention, he gives me a small smile. The lip-licker sneers at me and the salon girl says, "Did you go on a Birthright trip or Shorashim?"

"Neither. I went with my dad…He's Israeli."

"Oh," she says, then her friend boasts about her trip to Ireland with her Irish family.

While everyone talks about their adventures abroad, Avi reaches out and snakes an arm around my waist and pulls me toward him. "There's no chair for me," I say to him.

Guiding me onto his lap, he says, "Yes, there is." He taps the hair-flipper on the shoulder and I'm wondering if he wants to keep up the military talk until I hear Avi tell her, "This is my girlfriend, Amy."

While my heart opens up and loves Avi for telling a girl who's obviously hitting on him that he belongs to me, Miss Hair-Flipper gives me a small nod and turns her back to us to talk to another guy.

"Why is it every time I turn around another girl is talking to you?"

"I was talking to everyone, Amy. Don't be so paranoid. That guy over there, Dale, is from the South Side and that dude, Kyle over there, goes to your school. He wondered if I met you on an online dating service."

"What did you tell him?"

"I said he should get a life. Where's Jessica?"

"She left. It's kind of a long story," I tell him.

I guess I shouldn't be jealous of any other girl. I know how Avi feels about me. I guess a little part of me…that insecure part that shows its ugly head once in a while, knows the reality of it all. He's going back to Israel and I'm here. In less than twenty-four hours Avi will be back on a plane flying far away from me. And who knows what'll happen. I know what I want to happen, but how realistic is it?

"Don't look all serious, Amy," Avi tells me as he guides my chin down so I'm face to face with him.

Avi and I are in our little imaginary cocoon looking into each other's eyes as if no one else in the world matters.

A loud "Ahem" interrupts us.

Looking up, I'm shocked at the person standing in front of me. Okay, I knew Nathan was going to be playing tonight at the bar. But I didn't know that Nathan was going to transform into a rock star look-alike. His hair is spiked up, he's got eyeliner on, ripped faded jeans with a faded gray vintage T-shirt, and a black leather necklace hanging from his neck. I might add that he's not wearing glasses, either.

"Nathan?" I ask, not really sure if the guy in front of us is a Nathan look-alike or the real deal.

Nathan leans in and says to me, "The guys in the band call me Nate. And…well, this is *me*. You said to be *me*, right?"

Wow. Talk about going from geek to…wow. "Yeah."

When he leans back, I'm aware that Avi's grip has gotten tighter around my waist. I look down at my boyfriend, whose eyes are a little darker and intense like he's ready to fight for me.

"Avi?" I say.

He's still glaring at Nathan when he says, "What?"

"Look at me."

He does.

"Nathan's my friend, like a brother. Stop glaring at him like he's the enemy."

"I can't help it. Besides, if he's going to be your friend I liked it better when he wore glasses and the pants that were too short."

"Dude, don't be so lame," Nathan says. "The girl is in love with you. Or are you really all muscles and lack in the brain department?"

I feel Avi's muscles tense up, but before he can respond, I wrap my arms around his neck and hold him back. Luckily, the announcer starts introducing the band and Nathan is all too happy to jump up on stage and avoid another confrontation with Avi. I notice Nathan still has a cut and bruise from yesterday when Avi decked him.

"Nathan looks *so* hot, doesn't he?" Miranda says as Nathan, now the lead singer for Lickity Split, takes the mic. Okay, so he's the substitute singer for Lickity Split. It's not permanent, but it's still super cool.

Avi pulls me closer. "I never want you to look at him the way you look at me, Amy."

Nathan aka Nate Greyson puts the mic to his mouth, points to me, and says, "Amy, this one's for you."

What?

Did he just dedicate a song to me?

My arms are still around my boyfriend, and his arm

is still holding me tight while Lickity Split starts the loud music. Nathan belts out lyrics I've never heard before:

> She'll freak you out, she'll screw with your head
> She'll kiss you once, then leave you for dead

I stop listening after the word *dead*. Nathan and I are going to have a long talk about this song. It's too angry. Is Nathan angry? I'm sure with his past there's a lot of anger built up inside, but I can help him with that. Isn't that what friends are for? And to set the record straight I kissed Nathan twice, not once. And I did not leave him for dead. I knew after Avi kicked his ass last night he was alive…and left in very good care.

I shake my head and listen to the rest of the song. I can tell the crowd is getting into the lyrics and the fast beat. Nathan is a hit. The song tells the story about a guy falling for a girl who he thinks is playing games with him but in the end is just being herself. He realizes that the friendship is the real deal; the attraction was just a façade.

The mass of people in the bar are jumping up and down, shaking their heads to the song, and waving their hands in the air like crazy people. Or more like people who are totally engrossed in the beat and lyrics. Nathan aka Nate is jumping on stage like the rest of the crowd, getting totally into the song.

"Let's dance," Avi says loudly so I can hear over the speakers right near our table.

Me? Jumping around and head-banging? Yeah, I might do that in my room with nobody watching, but there's a bunch of kids from school here and I'm not used to losing control in front of an audience. "You go," I say, standing so Avi can mingle with the crowd. "I'm not the getting-sweaty-in-front-of-other-people kind of person." I'd rather he stay with me, but I'm not going to be the loser girlfriend who tells him what he can and can't do. If he's not afraid of people staring at him . . .

Avi stands and pulls me into the middle of the dance floor, which has become a pit of sweaty people drowning themselves in the music. Nathan is on his second song. This one is about rough times and even tougher times ahead. Very depressing, if I say so myself . . . and I'm a pessimist.

Avi starts getting into the music. The music is so loud I think my brain is rattling and we're all going to suffer brain damage and wake up deaf tomorrow morning. I can't stop watching Avi and how masculine and cool he looks while he's waving his fist in the air and moving to the pounding bass.

"Come on," he says. "Lose control with me."

Me, lose control? Not my style. Besides, if I jump around then my boobs are going to bob up and down like a buoy in the middle of a tsunami. I shake my head, refusing to make a spectacle of myself.

Scanning the people around me, though, makes me realize that I'm making a spectacle of myself by being the only one in the crowd right now standing still. Even Miranda is jumping around, waving her hands in the air like she's about to take flight. And she's got bigger and saggier boobs than me.

I start by bending my knees up and down. Looking over at Avi, his hair wet from sweat, inspires me. I take a tentative jump to test my new bra to see how bounce-resistant my boobs really are when they're strapped in tight. I look down as I take another test jump. The bounce rate is acceptable. But when I look up and see Avi's eyebrows furrowed as he watches me, I bite my bottom lip.

"People will stare at me," I try to explain over the loud music.

Avi shakes his head in frustration. "Let go, Amy. I want to see you without your inhibitions. If people stare, they're just jealous they're not having as much fun as you are."

I look down at my boobs.

His eyebrows go up. "Just try it," he says. "I dare you."

I do not take dares lightly, and he probably knows it. With a deep breath and determination I never knew was in me, I start jumping to the music and shaking my head around like Mutt after he takes a swim in Lake Michigan. Surprisingly, it feels good to let go and lose control for once.

The pit of people has gotten more crowded, I'm being pushed and pulled around by the mass of dancing maniacs. When I look up at the stage, Nathan is into his third song...or maybe his fourth. The words are seeping into my body:

> Fight the fight worth fighting
> Fight it to the death

Fight the fight worth fighting
And give up all the rest

As the words enter my consciousness, I wonder how many fights I've fought that weren't worth fighting. Nathan is totally into the performance. His face is fierce as he sings the words into the microphone. He's still trying to figure out where he fits in this world and why his parents gave him up.

When Nathan opens his eyes, he catches me watching him and winks at me before bending down and singing to some girl in the front row.

Soon the music stops and the band takes a break. While my ears adjust to the absence of blaring music, I head back to our table and plop myself down on an empty chair.

"You should let go more often," Avi says from behind me.

"I looked stupid," I say, which pretty much sums it up. Yes, I admit I had fun looking like a dork having my arms flailing and my boobs bopping around without caring what anyone thought. But in the end, I did look stupid. And in the end, I still do care what people think.

Avi bends down and kisses my neck. "You looked sexy, Amy."

"Will you two ever stop?" Nathan says as he joins our table.

I push Nathan away, but he's not paying attention to me. Something or someone at the other end of the bar is occupying him. I follow where his attention is focused.

"Bicky," Nathan whispers in shock.

The girl is even prettier in person and I hate her instantly. She has short, blonde hair pulled back with a headband and a half shirt showing off her amazing abs and bellybutton ring. And I swear her jeans must be painted on, they're hugging her body so tight. When I wear tight jeans I have to lie on my bed while I'm zipping them up. Bicky must have taken a dip in oil or grease in order to cram into her size zeros.

She sashays up to Nathan and puts her arms around his neck. "Aren't you going to introduce me to your friends?" she asks in a high, singsong voice.

Nathan is still in shock. His arms go slowly around her waist but he's looking at her like something isn't right. "What are you doing here? Did you break out of rehab?"

"You betcha." Bicky leans into him, almost tripping over her feet. "I heard you were performing. And besides, I wanted to meet the girl you kissed and wrote a song about." She looks me up and down. "You're her, aren't you?"

Oh, boy, am I busted. But before I can deny anything, Nathan says, "You're wasted, Bic."

"That I am, baby," she purrs, looking up at him. "You used to like getting wasted with me, until you turned all geek on me." She eyes his spiked hair and faded jeans. "Glad to see you're back to normal."

He grabs her wrists and pries her arms off him. "What we did wasn't normal, Bic. It was crazy and stupid."

Bicky is getting mad; her cheeks are red and splotchy and her eyes narrow into tiny slits making her look like an evil little pixie. "You used to like crazy and stupid, Nate. Or are you still going by Nathan? I can't keep up with all your personalities. Can she?" she says, pointing to me.

Everyone's eyes are on me now, analyzing my relationship with Nathan which is not good considering I just got back together with Avi.

"We're just friends," I blurt out, then hook my finger into Avi's belt loop making it obvious we're a couple. I hold my breath and peek at Avi's reaction to all of this.

Avi takes his hands off me, saying, "You don't have to defend yourself to me, Amy. I'll be at the bar while you work this out."

Is he serious? He doesn't have any doubts or insecurities about my friendship with Nathan? "You sure?"

"Yeah." He smiles and gives me a reassuring nod.

I watch his retreating back as he weaves his way through the crowd.

Wes, the guy from the Jewish youth group who helped me get Nathan in the band, weaves his way through the crowd. "Nate rocks, Amy. Thanks for bringing him by the other night. We're thinking of making him a permanent sub for Lickity Split."

"Cool," I say, but I'm not really paying attention to Wes or Bicky. Or Miranda, for that matter, even though she's in a deep conversation with a guy who I remember seeing at the youth group.

"Nathan…" I say, wanting to apologize for kissing him. I also want to tell him I'm sorry he has to deal with a screwed-up girlfriend on his first night singing with the band.

"It's cool, Amy."

"I can stay and help if you want."

"You've helped enough, bitch, don't you think?" Bicky slurs. I seriously think she wants to fight me, like in a physical fight. As I'm contemplating who would win in a fight between me and Bicky, I wonder if they teach tae kwon do in rehab. Because the only physical fight I've ever been in was with the sheep on the *moshav* last summer in Israel. And in the disco in Israel, but that was only because of the ear-licker—long story.

Bicky holds her hands out wide, "You want some of this?"

"Not really," I say. Is she joking?

Obviously not. My response really pisses her off, because now Nathan is trying to hold her back from charging me. I swear I'm living in the Twilight Zone. This girl seriously wants to deck me.

Not knowing what else to do, I close my fingers tightly into fists and hold them up by my face. The crowd around me starts moving backward. I think they're chanting "Chick Fight!" but I'm not sure. Whatever they're chanting, though, is fueling my bravery. Getting into the role, I start hopping around like boxers do. Maybe Bicky is too wasted and she'll fall to the ground on the first swing. It's wishful thinking, right?

If I break a nail I swear the chick is paying for a new manicure.

"You want some of this? Come and get me!" I say, playing the role while psyching myself up. I can seriously get into this, acting all tough and crazy. *Be afraid, everyone. Here comes the champion girl fighter of our time, Amy Nelson-Barak!*

From behind me, an arm snakes around my side and pulls me backward.

"What the...?"

I'm kicking whoever is holding me and punching at the arm, which is locked around me like a metal vice. Whoever it is drags me outside and sets me down on the sidewalk. I turn around and should have known nobody is as strong as my boyfriend who said he didn't want to deal with the drama, but ends up in the middle of it.

"What. Do. You. Think. You. Were. Doing?" Avi says each word slowly as if I'm an imbecile. His eyes are intense and his hands are shaking. I've never seen Avi shake before and it scares me.

"I'm sorry," I say.

He opens his hands out wide. "I leave you alone for two minutes and you're acting like a hellcat. How can I leave you for three years, Amy? I can't protect you while I'm in Israel."

I point to the club. "Bicky started it."

"So you took the bait?"

Uh, yeah. "What was I supposed to do, back down?"

"Yes," he says without hesitation.

"That's not me. Do you back down, Avi? Please tell me once in your life when you've backed down," I say, getting really riled up now because adrenaline is rushing through my body and I'm frightened because Avi's hands are still shaking.

No response.

Avi stares at his hands in horror, curses, then shoves them into the front pockets of his jeans. He swallows, looks away from me, and says, "Let's go."

I stay where I am, unmoving from this spot on the sidewalk in front of Durty Nevin's because I finally figured it out. What's making Avi shake.

His emotions are running rampant and he's not used to it.

Avi is a guy who is always in control of his body and mind. Even when I kidnapped him, he was in total control of the situation the entire time. Adrenaline he can handle, emotions he can't.

"You were afraid I was going to get hurt. That's why you're shaking," I blurt out.

He stops. His back is to me. "I don't shake."

"Then show me your hands."

"No."

"Avi, it's okay to be emotional."

"For you, maybe. But not for me."

I put my hand on his arm, knowing his pain about Micha's death is as raw in his chest now as it was when his brother first died. It has nothing to do with me and the fight. Avi can't let go of the pain of Micha's death, but still refuses to grieve. "You're only eighteen. And I hate to break the news to you, but you're human."

"I can't lose you, Amy," he says, his voice tense even though I sense he's trying to control his tone. "I came to America to prove to myself that I wasn't attached to you, that you weren't as important to me as my mind was telling me you were. I was wrong."

"You rode on a plane for twelve hours just to break up with me?" I say, totally confused and insulted now. I mean, seriously, to come all this way to prove I'm not worthy. "If that isn't the stupidest, most ridiculous, asinine thing I've ever heard," I say, then start walking across the street because I need space.

"A car is coming," he says.

Sure enough, I look behind me and a Honda Pilot is turning the corner and heads right to where I'm standing. "Aren't you going to save me?" I yell.

"Yeah, I am."

He walks fast to the curb and is about to step onto the street when I tell him, "If you take one step closer, it's over between us. I mean it."

"That car is gonna hit you," he says seriously, his eyes blazing with intensity. But he does stop cold in his tracks at the curb.

"They see me," I assure him.

Avi cocks his head to the side in confusion while his

hands come out of his pockets. He's trying to look relaxed, but I can tell he's ready to pounce and save me at any second.

"They'll stop," I say again, trying to prove a point that I'll be okay whether he's here to save me or not. He's not always going to be around to play Superman. Just like he wasn't around to save his brother when that bomber decided to kill innocent Israelis. My boyfriend is human and for once needs to let go and realize it.

Avi is looking at the car coming closer and then back at me. I can feel the struggle within him all the way over here. "Maybe they don't care," he says frantically to me. "Maybe they can't see you in the dark. Maybe the driver is drunk and—"

"Maybe I'll be okay, Avi."

"What if you're not? What if you die?"

I put my hand out. When the car reaches me, it comes to a halt. "Yo, chick, you gonna get out of the way?" a guy yells out the window.

"Everyone dies."

"Do you blame me for wanting to protect you, Amy? Now please get out of the street."

The guy in the car starts blowing his horn, really loud and it's hurting my already sensitive eardrums.

"I'm trying to teach my boyfriend a lesson," I scream at the driver. "Do you mind?"

"Yeah," he yells back. "Go teach him a lesson on Lower Wacker Drive where all the other wackos hang out."

"They give tickets for road rage in Chicago, you know," I say, then roll my eyes.

"Amy…I'm coming to get you in ten seconds."

"They give tickets for jaywalking in Chicago," the guy yells while intermittently beeping his horn. I get a little satisfaction he can't pass me because there's no room on the street.

"You have five more seconds to get your *ta'chat* over here."

"Do you love me, Avi?"

"Yes. Four seconds."

"Do you trust me?"

"Yes. Two seconds."

"Dude, if you don't get your crazy girlfriend out of my path I'm gonna move her myself."

"Amy," Avi says, closing his eyes tight and opening them again. Two seconds have come and gone. He has a pleading look in his eyes, eyes that are glassy with unshed tears. "*B'vakasha*. Please."

Okay, I give in. Because I've proven my point that I will be okay and Avi has proven that he can trust me. I walk over to him, my gaze never leaving his. The car screeches away. "You see. I survived."

His arms wrap around me, pulling me close.

"You're not shaking anymore," I say.

"I'm too angry with you to be scared."

"Angry? Listen, you've got to give up this superhuman theme going on in your life. Shit happens. *Life happens,* okay? You're leaving tomorrow and who knows what'll happen. Am I gonna sit around my room so nothing terrible can possibly happen to me? No. Are you going to sit in your army barracks and tell your commander you can't protect Israel because your crabby girlfriend will die if you get so much as a scratch on that perfect bod or face of yours? No."

"Stop talking so I can kiss you."

"You can't shut me up with kisses, you know."

"Wanna bet?" he says, smiling with those perfect white teeth while putting his perfect hands on my body as he lowers his perfect full lips to mine and proves to me he's right.

"Let's go back to your place," he says when we come up for air.

I'm holding on to his biceps for support because his kisses still make me feel drunk. "My *aba* is there. If you even kiss me he'll probably kill you first and ask questions later."

Back at the apartment my dad is nowhere to be seen. I check the messages. There's one from him saying he has to stay late for an emergency meeting. Then he says to make sure Avi is listening to the message, too, and the rest of the message is all in Hebrew.

I roll my eyes. "Is he having another sex talk?"

"Oh, yeah. Big time."

I stop the machine before the message finishes and give Avi a mischievous look. "What are you thinking?"

"Which rooms your dad has strategically placed the hidden cameras."

I laugh. "That's ridiculous. My dad doesn't have any hidden cameras in this house."

"He sounded pretty convincing, but I have an idea."

We get ready for bed, like a married couple except for the fact that we're just two trusting teenagers in complete love with each other. Avi's bed is still the couch in the living room, but this time I snuggle under the covers with him because my overprotective father isn't home watching our every move.

"I like this," I say. "So what's your idea?"

Avi pulls the covers over our heads so we're cloaked in complete darkness.

I finger his stubble with my fingertips. "This is your big idea?"

"It was either under the blanket or inside the hall closet."

"It's all *sababa*," I say, and Avi laughs.

"Yeah, it is."

I will tell you that under the covers was an excellent choice and VERY *sababa*, although I'm one hundred percent sure my dad does not have any surveillance cameras inside the house tracking our every move. I know this because although my dad came home an hour later and I ran to my room and pretended to be fast asleep, those cameras would have caught Avi and I in some very compromising positions despite our attempt to keep the covers over us.

Oh, don't get all worried…I'm still a pure seventeen-year-old. I'm just…well…more knowledgeable about certain things. (Things I'm more curious about now than I ever was.)

In the morning, Tarik picked up Avi and drove us all to the airport. I was crying the entire time, although I tried to keep it together. Our goodbye kiss held more promise than last time, although we both know we have to go on and live our lives. Don't ask, don't tell. We're going to take it one day at a time and see what happens. Hopefully this summer when I go to Israel it'll be the same as last night…well, without the fighting.

I purposely didn't bring up Jessica to Tarik, although now Tarik and I are sitting at Perk Me Up! and Jess could walk in at any time.

Marla brings me hot chocolate with the whipped cream overflowing because she knows how upset I am. Do you think my bloodshot, teary eyes give my upsetness away? Marla hugs me, a warm hug my mom would give me if she were here.

An idea pops into my head. I can't believe I hadn't thought of it before. "Marla, what do you think of my dad? You know, if he smiled more and got a good haircut?"

Marla laughs and walks back to the register, ignoring my question. I think I saw her blush a little, though. My dad loves her coffee; he never drinks it anywhere else. In fact, I think he got me this job just so he could see her more and have an excuse to hang out at Perk Me Up! Hmm…

The door to Perk Me Up! opens and guess who walks

in…yep, Jess. Along with Miranda and a very sad Nathan. Poor Nathan. Poor Jess.

It's time I stop making a mess of my own life and focus on everyone else. I can do it. There's nothing that says I have to be a Disaster Girl all the time. I can live a squeaky-clean life while helping others un-screwup their lives. No more getting in trouble for Amy Nelson-Barak.

My cell phone is ringing. It's my dad. "Hey, *Aba*, what's up?"

"What's up? Please tell me what a pair of plastic hand-cuffs are doing in the back seat of my car."

Oops. Everything is *so* not *sababa*.

About the Author

Simone was a teen in the 80s and still overuses words like "grody" and "totally," but resists the urge to wear blue eye shadow or say "gag me with a spoon." When Simone's not writing, she's speaking to high schools or teaching writing. In her spare time, she TiVos reality television and watches teen movies. She lives near Chicago with her family and two dogs.

Simone loves to hear from her readers! Contact her through her website at www.simoneelkeles.com.